Finale

-BOOK 10-

CRAIG HALLORAN

Finale
The Chronicles of Dragon: Book 10
By Craig Halloran
Copyright © September 2014 by Craig Halloran
Print Edition

TWO-TEN BOOK PRESS
P.O. Box 4215, Charleston, WV 25364

ISBN eBook: 978-194-1208-595
ISBN Paperback: 978-194-1208-601

http://www.thedarkslayer.net

Cover Illustration by David Schmelling
Map by Gillis Bjork
Interior Illustrations by Randy Linbourn
Edited by Cherise Kelley

Publisher's Note
This book is a work of fiction. Names, characters, places, and incidents either are the product of the author's imagination or are used fictitiously, and any resemblance to actual persons, living or dead, events, or locales is entirely coincidental.

NALZAMBOR
Key Location Guide

CHAPTER
1

NATH SLUNG HIS FISHING LINE into the stream. Wading in ankle deep, he could see fish swimming in the rippling waters but not taking the bait.

"Perhaps we should return," the commander said, standing behind him on the bank with his arms folded over his chest. "The skies darken. Rain comes."

Nath didn't reply. He had other things on his mind, particularly the rose blossom dragon that Selene had killed. And Selene as well.

"The High Priestess will not care for this, Dragon Prince," the commander added.

The man was very ominous underneath his dark helm. Peculiar, too. He'd stayed with Nath like a fly on glue.

Nath felt a nibble on his line and jerked his

wrist. A fish snapped up out of the water. "Got him!"

He swung the fish over the bank, hitting the commander in his chest plate.

"It's a big one," Nath said. "Ever fish before, Commander?"

"Certainly," the commander said, batting the fish aside. "Don't be foolish."

"Foolish," Nath said, cocking his head. "Did you call me—"

"Apologies, I meant no disrespect." He bowed. "A slip, Dragon Prince."

"Aw, don't call me that," Nath said. He grabbed the fish, poked inside its mouth, and pulled the hook out. "I'm hungry." He puffed a blast of fire, charring the fish. "Mmmm!" With his clawed finger, he gutted it, picked the meat off clean, and ate. "Want some?"

"No."

"Funny, I never notice you eating anything. You're a big man. I figure you eat plenty, too. Yet I never even hear your stomach growling."

"Runs in the family."

"Family, huh?" Nath said, chewing a mouthful. "Why don't you tell me about them? Do you have a wife? Did you marry with or without that ugly metal bowl on your head?"

"I don't have a wife."

"Tell me about your father and mother, then. Do they wear bowls on their heads?"

The commander shifted in his armor. His head twisted in other directions. He turned away and started walking up the bank.

Good.

There was something odd about the commander that Nath couldn't figure out, but he had other things on his mind. Selene. She'd been evasive. Normally, she stayed close by his side, but now she was distant. She had been ever since they had come out of the cave where she'd killed the rose blossom, the beautiful dragon that had attacked him along with the blue streaks.

Why did they attack me? Why?

He inspected his arms. Bands and streaks of white scales adorned them now. Even the patches of white in his palms had grown fuller. He glanced upward. A flock of dragons flew high in the sky in a V formation.

I should be up there.

He'd tried every day to turn into the dragon he'd once been, but he couldn't harness the magic. He didn't understand why. He snapped his fishing rod and tossed it into the water. "Bah." He glowered at the stream that rushed swiftly by. "Commander, any idea where we're headed? We seem to be doing circles."

The armored man came back his way and said from underneath the helm, "We go where the High Priestess says."

"Do you always do what you're told?"

"I follow orders."

"Have you ever not followed orders, say, when you were a boy?"

"Let's get back to camp," the commander said. "Perhaps you'll find the answers you seek there." The commander started to pass by.

Nath grabbed him in the nook of his arm.

"Let go," the commander said.

"Say, what is your name, Commander?" Nath said, nostrils flaring.

"You know that. I'm Commander Haan." He tried to pull away, but Nath held him fast.

"No, what is your first name?" Nath said, eyeing him. "And take off that helmet. How can you always wear such an ugly thing? Is your face so horrible that it must be hidden?"

Commander Haan stiffened and tried to twist from Nath's grip. He couldn't break it. He shoved Nath backward.

Nath shoved him back off his feet, onto the ground. "You're a big man, but don't be a fool, Haan." Nath stood over him. "Now, show me your face and tell me your name."

"No."

Nath's nostrils flared. His dander rose. Frustration set in. "Fine. I'll remove it myself, then."

CHAPTER 2

SELENE SOARED ABOVE THE CLOUDS with one thought in her mind.

Nath Dragon must die.

It didn't sit well. She'd have lost sleep over it if she slept at all, but that was always very little. Gorn Grattack had been clear. If Nath didn't turn to their side, then she was to bring him to Gorn, who would put Nath to death. Flapping her massive black wings, she streaked through the clouds.

A year ago, she'd have been thrilled to see Nath go. She would have killed him herself. She'd relished manipulating him.

But now, she'd gotten used to him. He was the only one like her, in so many ways: a black dragon who could also be human, the child of a powerful and distant father... She'd watched many die before, but such an outcome for Nath didn't seem possible. He had become large in her life.

She circled the skies, hour after hour. She'd marched her armies through the hills and beyond the valley on the longest path she could take toward Gorn Grattack.

She broke through the clouds again, dipping below their midst. Parts of the green lush lands were still intact, while other portions were dead and broken. The battle blood of men and dragons seeped into the ground all over, and the world trembled. The edges burned. Elves and orcs were in full battle. Dwarves marched out from Morgdon. The Legionnaires combed the lands. The races were restless, yet the Truce remained intact.

But it will not hold with Nath Dragon dead.

She glided to the earth and took her place on a spire in the mountains. Her keen dragon sight could pick up anything for miles. The forces of good were being spread out just the way Gorn Grattack had planned.

No more Nath Dragon. No more Truce. A new world will be ushered in.

Her black heart skipped a beat, and with a sigh, she puffed a plume of fire into the sky.

Gorn Grattack's will must be done. I will obey. Nath Dragon must die.

CHAPTER 3

"WHAT KIND OF MAN DOESN'T get hungry?" Nath said, reaching for Haan's helmet. "And doesn't sweat—or even stink, for that matter." He locked his fingers on Commander Haan's collar and started jerking at the dark helm. "Oof!"

Haan launched his metal gauntlet into Nath's belly, shoved him away, and rose up from his knee, reaching for his sword. "Stop this, Dragon Prince, I urge you."

Nath coughed and patted the iron-hard muscles under his scales. "You hit awfully hard for a mortal, too." He glared into Haan's hard eyes. "Harder than a big man even your size could. Explain that, and tell me what your name is." He pounced on the commander, smote him to the ground, and yanked off the helmet.

Haan cocked his arm back and struck Nath in the ribs.

Nath grimaced. "You can't hurt me when I'm ready for it. Now, who are you?"

Haan struggled.

Nath strained to hold him fast.

"Haan. Jason Haan is my name. Are you happy now?"

"No," Nath said. He groaned. "Still you don't sweat. How can that be?"

Haan's stern face grimaced under a head of short, black hair. His dark eyes shifted away from Nath's.

"Look at me," Nath demanded.

"No, I'll not." Haan flailed at him.

Nath grasped Haan's wrists and pinned them over the man's head. He squeezed the gauntlets until the metal bent and dug into flesh.

"How am I supposed to get those off now?" Haan said, rolling his eyes. "Sultans! Will you just let go of me—Nath. You're messing everything up."

Haan's voice had changed. No longer harsh and deep, it was lighter. And familiar.

Nath loosened his grip and leaned back.

Whop!

Haan's metal fist cracked him in the face. The big man effortlessly regained his feet and towered over Nath, to his dismay.

"Gorlee!"

Forming a sheepish grin, the big warrior nodded. "It's me." He reached down and pulled Nath up to his feet. "Sorry."

Nath rubbed his jaw. "Think nothing of it. If anything, I'm glad to see that kind of fight in you. But how long, Gorlee, how long?"

Gorlee scanned the surroundings.

"It's all right," Nath said, "no one is near."

Gorlee let out a breath, and his shoulders eased. "Good."

"Gorlee, how long have you been near? Have you been spying on me?

"Protecting you would be a better word."

Nath's eyes narrowed. Something didn't set with what Gorlee said. The way he said it wasn't right. "Sasha!" Nath stepped toward Gorlee. "That was you!" His hand lashed out, and his fingers locked around Gorlee's neck. "Why? Why?!"

"Keep your voice down," Gorlee managed to croak out. "Please." He clutched at Nath's arms. His face turned purple. "I can explain."

"How can you explain posing as my friend, looking me in the eye, and lying to me?"

"Please, Nath. I came to save you. Selene caught me, captured my essence, and made me her vessel." He choked. "I swear it."

Nath shoved him down.

For all Nath knew, Gorlee was still under her power. No matter what he did, she was there. How could he trust Gorlee now? How could he trust anyone? And what about Sasha? Bayzog? Where were they now?

Coughing, Gorlee started to speak. "Nath, you have to believe me. I'll tell you everything I know. And I know much. It's Selene."

"I don't want to hear it," Nath said. "I know she lies."

"It's more than that. She was ordered to turn you, and she failed. Do you know what that means?"

"Turn me?" Nath said. His anger subsided as confusion set in. "Turn me into what?"

Gorlee made his way to one knee, shaking his head.

"Into what, Gorlee? A draykis? Hah. I'm already a dragon. And I'm fully alive, not dead."

Gorlee swallowed as his eyes looked up.

"Kill me? And turn me into one of those monsters?"

"I believe it means something like that. It's very confusing."

"Why didn't you tell me this sooner?"

"I couldn't risk being discovered. I escaped. They still search for me, but I think I have them fooled, for now." He glanced around. "That's why you mustn't reveal my cover. We must play along."

"No. I must confront Selene about her plans for me," Nath said with a sneer.

"She's a liar, Nath. She'll twist your clear thoughts into the mud of worms."

"*You* are a liar."

"Not of my own volition."

"Hah, a changeling is nothing but a deceiver."

"Nath, you know me better than that."

"Do I?"

There was silence between them for a moment. Only the cool breeze that pushed down the tall grasses whistled by their ears. Nath had no one to trust now but himself. He grunted within. *I wish Brenwar was here.* He never had to doubt Brenwar. But even so, Gorlee's words had a ring of truth to them.

"Nath, there's more. The acolytes, they prepare for something. I fear Gorn Grattack is near."

Nath remembered his dream. The evil Dragon Overlord was coming for him, and he could feel a great presence of evil in his scales.

"So this is why Selene hesitates," he said, almost with a smile.

"Pardon?" Gorlee said, picking up his helmet.

Things fell into place. Selene's capture had been a ploy. Setting his jaw, he ground his teeth, clenching his fists.

"We need to keep this charade going, Nath," Gorlee said. "The way I see it, we need to get to the heart of the matter. That is Gorn. I was waiting for that moment. The moment to strike."

"And what exactly were you going to do? As I understand it, Gorn is every bit as powerful as my father."

"I was going to be your backup against him or Selene ..." He put on his helmet. "Let's play along while we can." He extended his hand. "I am your true friend, and I can explain much more later."

"I'd be interested to hear it." Nath stretched out his hand, but he still felt uncertain. A shadow grazed over the grasses. He jerked his head up. "Look out!"

The feline fury dropped out of the sky, right on top of the both of them..

Armored Draykis

CHAPTER
4

Nath felt the full weight of the feline fury on him. Its claws dug into his back. Peeled at his scales. He screamed. Out of the corner of his eye, he saw Gorlee pinned down underneath its other paw, wide eyed.

"Get off me," Nath said in Dragonese.

The beast stuffed his head into the dirt.

Nath pushed himself up, straining underneath its power and weight, inching his way up off the ground. "I said get off me!" Nath snarled.

The dragon cat clocked him in the back of the head with its horns.

Stars burst in bright spots before his eyes.

"Sultans of Sulfur!" Nath twisted underneath the cat dragon.

It pinned him down on his back, crushing his chest. Its jaw opened and struck.

"Gah!"

It bit down on his arm and flung him away.

He skipped over the ground and into the stream. Slinging his mane of auburn hair over his shoulder, he dashed the water from his eyes.

The feline fury was all over Gorlee. It ripped his armor off and dug its paws into his flesh.

"Great Guzan!" Nath blew a fireball into his hand and flung it at the monster.

The ball of flame exploded into its hide, and it let out a crying, cat-like howl, but it kept pounding away.

Gorlee was up on his feet. In a flash, he drew a gleaming blade from his scabbard. He flashed it at the fury.

It crawled backward, head low, yellow eyes shifting back and forth. They had it flanked.

Nath blew a fireball into each hand.

The feline fury's ears flattened on its head. It made an eerier howl. It crouched back, ready to pounce.

"You all right, Gorlee?" Nath said.

"I've a few hunks out of me, but nothing I can't heal. This beast, Nath, it's been hunting me for weeks." He stepped closer, slicing the blade through the air. "It will notify Selene, Nath. It seems I'm exposed. We both are, for that matter."

Nath figured Gorlee was right. If Selene found Gorlee, she'd kill him. If they killed the feline fury, she'd know that one of them was involved. Perhaps now was the time to make a break for it? No, with all the dragons and her army, it wouldn't take her long to hunt him down.

"Gorlee, I think it's time you left."

"What?"

"I'll handle the fury."

"No, Nath. We're in this together." Sword high, Gorlee advanced.

"No! Stop!"

Gorlee froze.

The feline fury drew back, ready to spring at any moment.

Nath flicked the balls of flame into the rippling water. They sizzled and disappeared. He kneeled down, eyeing the dragon cat. Summoning a power he felt deep inside, he said in Dragonese, ""Come. Come, great dragon cat. I'm a friend. You should know that," Nath added, lying flat on the ground.

"Nath, what are you doing? He'll gore you."

Growling at Gorlee, the feline fury eased out of its stance and slunk closer to Nath.

Nath spread his arms wide and welcoming. "Come, great dragon cat. Come." He felt power. A connection with the dragon. Something he'd not felt before. Unlike Selene's other dragons, the feline fury had a cunning mind of its own, no longer under the influence of a spell or jaxite stones. He stretched his fingers out as the beast inched closer. "Come, friend."

"Nath, get away. You're mad," Gorlee said in a loud whisper.

Nath felt the tips of the dragon cat's whiskers and its lava-hot breath on his face. Its citrine-colored cat eyes bore into his. A purr rumbled in its great scaled belly, and it lay down beside him and licked his hand.

"I'll be," Gorlee said.

Nath smiled at Gorlee. "Father once told me, 'You'll never make new friends unless you try.'"

As the dark clouds rolled over the skyline, Nath headed back toward camp, heavy in thought.

Is Selene really going to kill me?

Gorlee had made his case, filling in details Nath hadn't known. The ruse of Gorlee posing as Sasha in order to gain his trust had infuriated him, but he believed Gorlee now. The changeling had no reason to lie. But how would he deal with Selene?

The feline fury nuzzled past him and took to the air.

"Are you certain that beast is on our side now?" Gorlee said, marching at his side. "It nearly ripped me apart a few times."

"Me too," Nath said. "But he's an ally now. He's made his choice. He just needed a reason, and now he has one." He frowned. "Poor creature. All these years, Selene kept him through fear, rearing him for wrong, but a little kindness, a tad of submission turned him."

"Do you think that will work with the rest of the dragons that want to tear out our throats?"

"Probably not."

They walked on, pushing along the path, less than a mile from the main camp now. Inside, Nath simmered. He'd been manipulated. He'd trusted in the Truce, and now he knew it was all a lie. A ploy to keep him on the sidelines. Selene had used him to fool everybody, and it had worked quite well.

"Nath," Gorlee said. "I'm sorry."

"For what?"

"Deceiving you as Haan."

"It wasn't your fault, Gorlee."

"I was foolish," the changeling said.

"You were brave. Don't start doubting yourself now, Gorlee. You risked your life for me. For the land. That's ... well, that's something." He slapped his hand on Gorlee's shoulder. "That's the mark of a true friend."

"Thanks Nath," he said. "So, do you really think we can fool her?"

"I don't see why not. After all, you fooled me. Plus, now we have another ally in the fury. I think it will be a good one. We'll see." Still, something stirred in Nath's belly. He needed to be at full power, and he hadn't been for quite some time. Not since he'd flown that first time.

Selene has done something to me. Hah! I'm a fool not to have realized that.

Heavy raindrops began to pelt them from above. Soon the path became muddy. Gorlee kept chattering about things. He talked about Bletver the triant. Even Nath hadn't heard of such a creature. Gorlee also told him about the heroes in the tavern, the ones who fought in the name of Balzurth. It made Nath's chest swell. Men, the most unpredictable of all, fighting in the name of his father did his heart good.

"Things are going to have to come undone soon, Nath. The farce called a truce must end. I think that's on you."

It seemed sacrifices were being made all over. Nath felt like everyone gave something but him. He frowned as Gorlee continued speaking. He couldn't stop thinking about Brenwar, Ben, Bayzog, and Sasha. Did they still even live?

As they reached the edge of the camp, a group of acolytes, tattooed and bald, greeted them. "You must come with us, Dragon Prince."

"Why?" Nath said. "Has something happened?"

"Peace Bringer," said another acolyte, "High Priestess Selene has an urgent summons. She awaits you in her tent."

"I see. All right, then." He glanced at Gorlee, but the helmet on his friend's head hid any expression. "Let's go then." He nodded as he left. "Commander."

CHAPTER 5

"I SEE YOU ARE WELL," NATH said to Selene.

She wore all-black robes traced in gold. Her crown of silver leaves was on her head. She took a seat at a long table inside the tent. There was no one else there but them.

"Please have a seat, Nath. Eat with me."

"I'm not hungry." He took a place at the table and pushed a plate of steaming food away.

"Interesting," she said, placing her cloth napkin on her lap. She took a sip of wine. "Not drinking either, I imagine."

"I'm fine." His stomach rumbled.

Her eyebrows lifted. "Are you sure about that?"

"Probably some fish I must have eaten too fast."

"Fish?" She tapped her fingernail on the glass goblet. "All right, then."

"Selene, what is this all about? You summoned

me, after all, not I you. As a matter of fact, I've hardly seen you in days." He draped his elbow over the back of his chair. "Why is that?"

With a look of sadness, she scooted her plate away, rested her elbows on the table, and locked her fingers together. "Nath, I've been avoiding something."

"Is that why you march this army in circles?"

"So you've noticed."

"I know the land as well as anyone." He looked at his clawed fingers. "So why is that? Hmmm? I think you are avoiding Gorn Grattack."

She raised her head. "Why would you think that?"

"We've had many conversations, Selene. And you've made it pretty clear that you don't care so much for him. I seem to recall you mentioning that the two of us could defeat him."

"Oh," she said with a small smile, "did I say that?"

"You know you did," he said. "And I believed you."

"Believed?"

Careful what you say, Nath. She still has to believe she has you duped.

"Yes. Selene, I think you felt we could take Gorn down together, but now ... well, now you doubt me. After all, I can't even turn into a dragon, and I showed mercy to that rose blossom that wanted to kill me." He shrugged. "Maybe you fear I don't have the killer instinct needed to carry out a fight with the likes of Gorn—"

She held up her palm. "Let's not say his name too many times. His name evokes attention."

"I see. So, am I right?"

"You are wise as a serpent."

"Of course, we still have my father's forces to contend with. They are liable to make another attempt on your life, and we can't let that happen. Not if we're going after, well, you know who."

Selene stared at him with silence. Finally, she said, "I admit I am surprised."

Not as surprised as I am. I can't believe she's swallowing this.

They marched onward, mile after mile, league after league. Nath and Gorlee rode on horseback side by side, Gorlee's lips silent under the ominous metal helm that he wore. Behind them was the rest of the army, troops numbering in the thousands now, their bootsteps splashing through sloppy mud holes. The heavy rain rang off their metal armor. It made for a dreary sound, creating an unforgiving itch down Nath's spine.

Am I a fool, rushing headlong into the mouth of Gorn Grattack?

And there was Selene.

Why would I believe anything she said? She lied every time before. Does she really want to face Gorn Grattack now?

Faith urged him forward. He didn't know why, but he had to move on. Confront his fears. Face Gorn Grattack and save the world or doom it. He'd been looking inward for quite some time. Perhaps that was his biggest problem: fear of failure.

Am I to let the world down the same as I did my father?

It ate at him, the thought of not seeing his father again—nor Dragon Home. Nor any of his friends, for that matter.

Guzan! I wish Brenwar were here. He'd be fired up for this final battle.

He glanced at Gorlee.

At least I'll have one friend to witness my death. I hope it's a grand funeral.

CHAPTER

6

"HIT 'EM!" BRENWAR YELLED. HE hefted up a rock as big as himself. "Now!" With a heave, he hurled the huge missile through the air.

Beside him, Ben nocked an exploding arrow, took aim, and fired.

Twang!

Coming right for them was a hull dragon, bright green and orange scaled, more than thirty feet in height, stomping through the valley.

Brenwar's boulder rocked it in the jaw.

Ben's arrow skewered its neck.

Boom!

The massive monster staggered backward and let out an ear-splitting roar.

Ben fired again.

Boom!

Brenwar ripped another hunk out of the ground and said, "Quit showing off!" He chucked it. The rock smashed off the monster's nose. "Perfect hit!"

With an important look on his face, Pilpin picked up a smaller rock and threw it at the hull.

Around Ben's arrow, the hull sucked in a mouthful of air.

"Uh oh," Ben said, "here it comes!"

"Bayzog!" His head whipped around. "Where are you, elf?"

A bluish-green light glowed to life inside the dragon's great maw.

Brenwar and Ben glanced at one another.

Pilpin made as if to advance on the hull.

"Take cover!" Brenwar yelled, snatching Pilpin by the collar.

"Where?" Ben said, looking around.

The hull dragon's scales charged with light. Mystic fire dripped from its jaws.

Bayzog dropped from the sky with the Elderwood Staff in hand. "Get down!" he commanded.

Whoooooooosh!

A firestorm of energy erupted from the dragon's mouth.

With a wave of Bayzog's hand, a great wall of yellow mystic energy formed, shielding them all. The torrential flames sizzled angrily against the wall. Sparks and specks of bright energy burst in the air. Bayzog's stern face beaded in sweat.

Brenwar could feel the intense heat through his armor. "Get out of there, elf, before it roasts you alive!"

The geysers of flames came on. The shield started to pop and crack.

"Run!" Bayzog said. "Run!"

"I'm not running!" Brenwar picked up his war hammer. "Forward. Onward," he said, still holding Pilpin back by the collar. He wound the hammer up, spinning it like a pinwheel.

The shield crackled and wobbled. Bayzog drifted to the ground. Flames spilled through the shattered holes, setting fire to his lily-white robes.

"Mrurumrah Hooooooooooo!" Brenwar bellowed. Then, with all of his bracer-enhanced might, he let the ancient hammer fly. It burst through the shield and straight through the flames. A great clap of thunder popped the air and shook the ground.

Kra-boooooooom!

Bayzog's shield dissipated, and the dragon's fiery breath was gone, leaving only a smoky mist that covered almost everything.

Somewhere in the mist, the hull dragon made an awful moan, and a tremendous *thud* shook the ground.

Brenwar scurried forward and lifted Bayzog back up to his feet.

"I better not have lost my hammer."

Bayzog dusted off his robes. "I didn't think dwarves ever lost anything."

"Hrmph," Brenwar and Pilpin both said.

The four of them stood on the cliff's edge in silence. A stiff breeze cleared the air, revealing the monstrous form of the hull dragon collapsed on the earth. Trees and branches were crushed beneath it.

"Do you think you killed it?" Ben said, leaning over the edge.

"Why don't you go down there and tickle it?" Brenwar said. "Or pinch its scales, maybe."

The great monster didn't stir, not in the slightest. It was tons of scales and muscle, with great armored fins on its back, wingless and formidable. Brenwar looked at the bracers on his wrists, the ones that Balzurth had gifted to him. They pulsed with an eerie yellow light. It gave him a rush. Filled him with power. With the war hammer and the bracers, he felt like he could take out an entire mountain. With the hull dragon down, he practically had.

Filling his lungs full of air, he pounded his chest and let out a tremendous bellow.

"Hooooooooooooooooooooooo!"

"What are you doing?" Ben said, covering his ears. "Are you trying to wake it?"

Brenwar's great voice continued to fill the valley as he broke out in song.

"*Home of the Dwarves! Morgdon! Home of the*

31

dwarves! Morgdon! We have the finest steel and ale! Our weapons will never fail! Morgdon!"

"Look," Bayzog said, pointing down at the great dragon.

Brenwar stopped and looked.

The hull dragon was moving.

"By my beard!" His brows buckled as his eyes scanned for his war hammer. "Fetch my weapon, mage!" he yelled at Bayzog.

The dragon snorted a blast of smoke and let out an angry groan.

"He looks mad, Brenwar," Ben said, loading up Akron. "I don't think he likes your singing."

"Aw, shut it, human," Brenwar said, scraping a hunk of stone out of the earth. The sound of hooved feet caught his ears, and he stopped.

Shum and Hoven galloped by, holding up spears at least eight feet long. Dragon Needles.

"Don't you dare kill my dragon!" Brenwar shouted, but they were gone.

Each Roamer leapt off his horse and climbed up the dragon. Without hesitation, they rammed their Dragon Needles into the dragon's armored chest. The tips pierced the thick hide and plunged straight into the heart.

The dragon's bright eyes glared with intensity. It lurched a few times, but then the eyes went dim.

Brenwar was furious. In a rush, he stormed down

the hillside and greeted the Roamers alongside the dragon, shaking his fist at them.

"That was my dragon!"

Shum twirled his Dragon Needle around—once, twice, three times—shrinking it. Looking over his shoulder, he said, "You can still have it. Just so long as you remember it was us who killed it."

"Why you pointy eared, fat—"

Shum lowered the tip of his spear in Brenwar's face. "Watch what you say, dwarf."

Brenwar slapped it away. "Don't ever stick that stick in my face again, pot belly!" He stormed away and scoured the valley until he got his hands back on his war hammer. He hugged it to his chest and stepped alongside the head of the hull dragon. Its magnificent horn was cracked off at the top of its head, which had a dent in it. "You did that, not them," he said to the war hammer. "Dragon Needles? Pah."

CHAPTER
7

"NO SMILES? NO JOY?" SASHA said. "You men should be happy. You saved another town."

Brenwar and Pilpin each snorted a grunt. Shum and Hoven remained expressionless, and Bayzog's face was creased in concentration.

"I'm happy," Ben said, tossing some firewood into the smoking pit. "Who wouldn't be, after surviving a battle with a monstrous dragon? Woo, I'm relieved!" He stirred the fire with a stick and rubbed his beard. "Don't pay any mind to those sour faces over there. Especially the bearded ones."

"I'd be happy, too, Mother," Rerry said, stepping out of the woodland and dropping a stack of sticks on the ground, "if I'd gotten a few licks in on that hull dragon." He drew his sword. Lightning-quick strokes cut the air. *Swish. Swish. Swish. Swish.* He slammed the blade back inside his scabbard. "But again I missed it, thanks to Samaz. I can't always be his keeper, you know."

Bayzog spoke up. "You did well, Son. It was your duty."

"Does it always have to be my duty? After all, he's older. He should be watching over me and not me over him. I sicken of it, Father. I want to fight, not sit watching Glum Face all the time."

Bayzog lifted his eyes to the sky, shaking his head. The stars and moon twinkled behind the drifting clouds, but that wasn't all. Winged silhouettes drifted through the sky, sending a chill through him. He noticed Shum and Hoven glancing upward as well. "Sasha, how about you conceal these flames?"

Warming her hands, she was just about to sit down beside him when she paused and kissed him on the head. "I'd love to."

She scratched up a handful of dirt from the ground, rubbed it in her hands, and began muttering a quick incantation. Tossing the dirt into the air, where it sparkled bright with energy, she said, "Azzah!"

A dimness formed over them, stretching from tree limb to tree limb.

"Well done," Bayzog said. He took her by the hand and kissed her. "I couldn't do better myself."

"I know," she giggled as she took her place

beside him. She clasped her warm hands around his. "Some things take a woman's touch."

"Like your cooking," Ben piped in. "Please don't let Brenwar and Pilpin make supper again. It tasted like baked bark."

Pilpin tossed a metal pot in the fire and chomped his teeth. "You cook, then. We don't need as much food as you anyway, do we Brenwar?"

Brenwar groaned in agreement.

Rerry plucked the pot out of the fire and tossed it back and forth until the metal cooled, saying, "I'll make it. Something with some elven zeal will lift these dour spirits." He patted his belly. "And I'm too hungry to wait for all this bickering to end." He walked away with a sigh.

Bayzog could feel something he didn't like: pressure. There was fatigue in everyone's movements. Heavy concern in their faces. None more so than Brenwar's. Losing his charge, Nath Dragon, had unsettled the ever-stout dwarf. He'd been edgy ever since Nath took things into his own hands. It left everyone uncertain.

"How much farther, Shum?" Bayzog said.

The ranger was sharpening his elven blade with a rune-faced whetstone while Hoven hummed a gentle tune. "A few more days. You'll see. The land starts to decay. Darken. Leaves fall from the trees out of season. I assume there'll be more encounters on our way. Let's hope we can avoid most of them."

"That hull dragon was unavoidable, that much is certain," Ben said. "It was its own city. Do you think there will be more hulls? I'm running low on exploding arrows."

"Then take better aim with them," Brenwar growled. "Unless Bayzog can conjure up more."

Bayzog shook his head.

"Oh," Ben continued, "maybe I need some practice. Why don't you put an apple on your head and let me shoot it?"

"You'd like that, wouldn't you?"

"Other than it being a shame to waste a good piece of fruit, why yes, I think I would." Ben chuckled.

Brenwar folded his arms over his chest and said, "Pah. All you do is waste arrows and your breath."

Pilpin barked a laugh.

Bayzog tuned them out. They'd gone on like this for hours, but it wasn't the worst thing. It kept an edge about them, and they needed that. It had taken Sasha some time, but she'd gotten used to it. He squeezed her hand. She looked over and smiled at him. Regardless of the darkness, doubt, and despair that surrounded them, she seemed happy.

"I'd better go check on Samaz," he said. "It's been awhile. Would you like to come along?"

She stroked his long black hair, rubbed his back, and said, "No. I'll help Rerry prepare our supper. He's a horrible cook, but he tries. You go. Take all the time you need with our quieter son."

"Save me some stew." He patted her knee and departed.

Samaz sat cross legged out on the end of a rocky crag. The stiff breeze bristled his short black hair and played with his robes, which were snug around his body. He didn't turn as Bayzog approached. Instead, his chin was tilted up and his eyes were glassy and dreamy.

Of all the things I've dealt with, this always seems the most strange.

Samaz had always been like this. He'd sit up in his bed, late at night, eyes open, staring at nothing yet everything.

I'd love to see what's in that mind of his.

Quietly, Bayzog eased down into sitting position. It was best not to disturb Samaz from his slumbers. He'd broken Rerry's wrist for it once. It was no wonder the brothers bickered so much and Rerry resented him.

Bayzog crossed his legs the same as Samaz, closed his eyes, and relaxed. They used to do this all the time, have long whiles of peace and quiet. It soothed him, and he was certain it brought comfort to Samaz as well. His thick-set son, though aloof and distant, no doubt knew he was there. Samaz had amazing intuition. Rerry could never sneak up on him, nor beat Samaz at hide and seek, either.

The crickets chirped, and the distant pixies played. Bayzog could feel his elven roots stretching out and acclimating to the sound of the woods: the rustling of branches, hooves that scurried through the night. He'd gotten more in tune with his elven roots over the past twenty-five years, and it had been good. He started to breathe easy. His taut shoulders relaxed. He became one with his son. One with nature.

Moments went by.

"Father," Samaz said, softly.

Bayzog opened his eyes, turned, and faced his son. Samaz's features were covered in sweat, and his dark eyes were wide. Placing his hand on his son's chest, he felt the young part-elf's heart pounding.

Thump-thump ... thump-thump ... thump-thump ...

Unable to hide his worry, he asked, "What is it, Son?"

A silvery tear dripped down Samaz's cheek. His body trembled. "I–I saw a dragon die." He pointed toward the sky.

Bayzog followed his finger.

A large black object dotted the sky, blotting out a small part of the rising moon. It sent a shiver through Bayzog. He stood up, and his slender jawline dropped. It was too big to be a dragon, yet it moved too slowly to be anything else, and something propelled it forward, dragging it over the mountain treetops.

"What is that, Samaz?" He shook his son by the shoulders. "Have you any idea?"

Teary eyed, Samaz spoke again, his voice more haunting this time. "I saw a dragon die." He looked at Bayzog. "I saw Nath Dragon die."

CHAPTER 8

THE GREEN AND COLORFUL FIELDS were in a state of decay. Leaves fell from branches. Branches fell from trees. At night, the pixies no longer sang.

Nath stood in the morning mist and sighed. His clawed fingertips tingled. He felt tired. He never felt tired.

"Time to move," said Gorlee, posing as Jason Haan. He was buckling his armor over his big frame. His sullen face with its hard eyes showed no sign of worry. "Seems we're getting closer to something."

"Yes," Nath said, donning a leather tunic Selene had given him. It was plain, with no insignia of Barnabus, which was odd, seeing how everyone else was marked. It did have a special crest on it, a crown resting on wings. "I'm curious as to what that something is."

He was speaking of Gorn Grattack.

Gorlee came closer, careful no one else was within earshot, and said, "It's not too late to move on."

"Nervous?"

"I feel something I cannot describe."

"Does it make you feel any better that I feel the same way?"

Gorlee managed the grimmest of smiles on his warrior's face. "It does."

"Good then. Now listen, Gorlee. I'd just as soon you left to go find our friends Brenwar and Bayzog. You of all people have the best chance of coming out of this, and the fury no longer hunts you. I'd just as soon you slipped out, first chance you got. Someone else will have to fight this war if I fail."

"I wish you wouldn't say such things," Gorlee said, buckling on his helmet.

"Things need to be clear."

Without another word, Nath mounted his horse, and Gorlee followed suit. The army finished breaking down the camp, loaded up, and was on the move again. Through the misty rain they went, mile after mile, league after league.

Nath felt incomplete. He forged on through his doubts. Could he trust Selene at all? Could he trust himself? He'd made plenty of bad decisions. The Truce he had agreed to might have been the worst of them all.

But I couldn't let my friends die, even though they were willing to. What kind of friend would I be if I had let them die?

He must not have done the right thing, though, because the farther they went, the smaller he felt inside.

Near evening, when they were cresting a hill made up of fallen trees and dried-up and broken branches, Selene appeared. She rode on the back of a dark grey horse. Her robes were deep violet woven in red, and her black dragon tail hung over both sides of the saddle. Draykis were on either side of her.

"We are near, Nath," she said, coming along his side and leading him away. "Come." She glanced at Gorlee and then spoke to the draykis commanders. "Stay here with the rest of the army. We shall return. Wait."

Without a glance back, Nath followed Selene through the barren mountain range. It was a territory he was unfamiliar with. They would be hard pressed to push an army along this pathway, which cut through a thick comb of briars, thickets, and dying trees. And even though the forces of Barnabus were anything but his kind of people, he felt abandoned without them. A little more so without Gorlee in tow.

No one watching my back now.

Ahead, Selene rode tall in the saddle as always. She had a gentle sway in her body as she rode, plodding along, patient, eyes forward. The tip of her tail lay flat over the saddle. Sometimes he noticed that it would whip back and forth, caress her hair, or coil along her waist. Not now.

She's nervous? Perhaps she is *on my side.*

After miles of riding through the dank day, she stopped her horse and looked back at him. "Are you ready?"

"There's never been a moment that I wasn't," he said, smiling weakly.

"Huh," she said, dismounting. "We'll leave the horses here. Are you all right with that, or are you more comfortable around pets?"

Nath slid off his horse and hitched the reins over a branch. "Walking is fine by me, company or not." He stretched out his long arms, rolled his shoulders, and cracked his neck. He puffed a ring of smoke. "I'm ready to greet him."

Selene came closer and locked her arm around his. There was a warm-soft texture to her scales. Standing almost as tall as he, she looked up into his eyes. "Don't do anything rash."

"Me?"

"Just keep your tongue in place and let me do the talking. Follow my lead."

"Silence and inaction aren't my better qualities."

"No, no they aren't. But it's your life, Nath. Your actions will determine how much longer you keep it."

He squeezed her hands and held them to his chest. He wasn't sure why. He just did it.

She didn't resist.

That's when he said to her, "Isn't your life worth something, too?"

"I can live with my choices, Nath. I've lived for them. I'll die for them. Not even you can change that."

The morbid statement created a void inside him.

Her fingers slipped out of his, and she walked away, tail dragging over the path.

An ominous dragon-woman puzzle, that's what she is. If I live, I might just write a poem about this.

CHAPTER 9

GORLEE FIDGETED INSIDE HIS ARMOR. He was of no use to Nath now. Selene had him. His effort to stay close had been blocked. They'd been gone for hours, and darkness had come.

"Get back with the rest of the troops," one of the draykis commanders hissed. He had great black wings on his back, and he was very tall and ominous inside his patchwork of metal armor. "We'll watch the pass."

"I don't recall the High Priestess removing my authority. I'm to watch after the Dragon Prince, so far as I can."

"There is nothing to watch now," the draykis said, looking down the path Nath and Selene had taken. "But soon, I'm certain, there will be a funeral."

"Until I see a body, I'm just fine right where I am."

The draykis grabbed Gorlee's horse by the harness and jerked its neck. The horse nickered.

"Ride your beast away," it said. "This army is under the watch of the draykis now, not men."

Gorlee looked into its face of scales and beady eyes and said through his teeth, "Let ... go."

"Move along, human," the draykis said, releasing the harness and walking away. "Huh-huh, move along. There are four of us and just one of you, and any one of us can tear you in two."

Gorlee didn't doubt he meant it. Very few mortals could handle draykis. But he wasn't mortal. He clenched the reins of his horse and nudged it away.

"Enjoy your sleep, human, while we who need no sleep watch over things. Huh-huh," it said, following with a hiss.

Gorlee moved deeper into the ranks, where the army made camp. There was little reason to begin a scuffle with the draykis. After all, they were Selene's most trusted. Them, and a handful of acolytes. He'd been clever enough to fool her. He had fooled them all, taking on the identity of Jason Haan. Selene and the draykis didn't pay much attention to the men in the ranks. She'd grouped the different races of followers among themselves. In the ranks were goblins, orcs, gnolls, and men as hard as you'd ever meet. Fat, big, ugly, or rangy, they fought for greed. Gold. A twisted form of glory. Now he sat among them, listening to their coarse talk. Their usual tone, one of ruthless mirth, was now replaced by a dull sort of melancholy. It seemed that the draykis weren't the only ones pushing them around. So were the other races, not to forget the lizard men.

"They're showing their colors," one man said. His scarred face was shadowed in the fire. "Pushing us around."

"The orcs have been hoarding our rations."

"The goblins slide away with our steel," said another man, whose beard hung to his knees. "I caught one with a quiver of my arrows and throttled him." He looked up at Gorlee. "Commander Haan, may I ask what in Narnum is going on?"

Gorlee didn't have the answer to that. The truth was he'd been more concerned about Nath. But he was aware that some of the captains, the human ones, had been kept out of some of the meetings. It happened from time to time, but of late it had been more frequent. "Don't fret. I'll speak with the acolyte chiefs at first light."

The bearded man spit a wad of tobacco on the ground and looked into the sky, shaking his head. "Something is not right about this," he muttered.

All the others continued to mumble and grumble and complain among themselves.

Gorlee didn't entirely understand it all, but he'd been around the races long enough to know that humans weren't born with as much wickedness as the other kinds. They just had an unpredictable flair about things.

He started away toward the edge of the human camp and took a walk. The entire time, he was listening to the other races. After all, he understood all their languages. Languages were second nature to him. He didn't hear much, however. The boisterous orcs were quiet. The gnolls gnawed on bones. The goblins stitched up their crude armor and painted themselves with bright, ghastly images. And the lizard men, who talked little at the best of times, now hardly breathed a hiss.

Gorlee kept walking, keeping his distance, but he could feel their eyes on him. The night air with its dripping rain contributed to an already very heavy tension.

Something is wrong, he thought. *Very, very wrong.*

He wondered if he'd been discovered. Perhaps Selene had known his identity all along. Maybe the feline fury had tipped her off after all. The dragon cat was as cunning and quick as any dragon. He tried to shake the feeling. Rubbed his hands together. He felt chilled.

Perhaps it's time to change. Surely I can make off

through the woods as something undetectable. Nath Dragon needs my help.

A commotion caught his ear. A small group of goblins barreled their way into the human camp, carrying torches and making a fuss. In an instant, a crowd of angry men gathered around the goblins, shouting.

Gorlee pressed his way into the throng. "What's going on?" he yelled. "Get out of my way, men!"

The surge of bodies didn't part. Instead, the knot of men tightened, and their voices became angrier. Standing taller than all of them, Gorlee could see the goblins standing in the middle of the fray, screaming and waving their torches back and forth. They yelled in Goblin. Gorlee's blood froze as he recognized the words they said.

"Kill them, dragons! Kill them all!"

Suddenly, a large ring of dark shadows dropped from the sky, surrounding the human camp. The dragons, bigger than horses, spread their wings, corralling the dumbfounded men. Gorlee heard a sharp draw of air fill all the dragons' lungs. The dragons' eyes glowed with light, and he screamed, "Get down! Get down!"

Bright red-orange flashes roared from their mouths, setting fire to everything. To everyone. Including himself.

"No! Stop! What are you doing?"

The sound of agony. The intense heat. The horrid scramble of bodies overwhelmed him.

CHAPTER 10

THE PATH BOTTOMED OUT. SELENE stopped. The valley ahead was a barren half moon, surrounded by more mountains. Nath's stomach became a little queasy as the stench of decay riled the air.

"What is this place?" he said to Selene.

Ahead, towering stones that only giants could have lain jutted out of the ground. They stood upright in a pattern, though some of them had fallen long ago. Many were coated in vines, and some of the blocks were covered in moss and weeds. Nath figured if he could fly and look down on them, the stones would spell out something.

"More temple ruins," Selene said, taking a few slow steps forward. "I think you are familiar with them."

Nath was, but these were bigger. Some of the

stones stood as high as forty feet. He noticed that on some pairs of them, other great stones rested on top, forming massive gateways. It would take a hundred horses, maybe more, to move any one of them. He followed Selene, noting the ancient rune markings on the stones. He was familiar with the ancient use of portals. The scales on his neck tingled.

"This isn't your typical ruin," he said, looking up at the top of one. A live dragon with a slithering tongue sat perched up there. A grey scaler. Its glowing green eyes narrowed on him.

Nath's eyes narrowed back. "He *is* here, isn't he?"

"You can feel him," Selene said. "Can't you?"

Dark power. Deep. Penetrating. Suffocating. Evil. It would have taken a man's breath away, dropped the stoutest warrior to his knees. A mist drifted over his ankles, hugging his scales and giving him a chill. Above, he noted more dragons perched on the stones: grey scalers, sky raiders, iron tusks, copper hides. The moonlight twinkled off their scales and claws.

"I hate to admit it, but I almost can't feel at all."

But the feeling wasn't unfamiliar to him, either. There had been days when he'd had to face his father, Balzurth, knowing he had done wrong. The power that radiated from Balzurth was unimaginable sometimes. At times, it seemed his father's mere thoughts could shake the room.

Nath swallowed. Summoned up his courage. Now he was facing a power just as great but unfamiliar. A power that wasn't warm and fiery, but instead an icy breath of death.

He then heard his father's voice inside his head. *"You can have faith in me or in your friends, but don't forget to have faith in yourself, Nath."*

"Are you scared, Nath?" Selene said, glancing back at him. "I think I see fear in your eyes. It worries me."

"And I note a tremble in your voice," he said, pulling back his shoulders and stepping to her side. "But I'd be lying if I said didn't feel fearful."

"Fear is good. It can give us an edge."

"Us?"

She didn't say anything, but it felt like a slip. A good one, the kind that gave his spirits a lift. Maybe Selene wasn't going to double-cross him? He took a deep, silent breath through his nose and into his chest, stoking the dim fires within. Onward he went with Selene, through the network of colossal stones where dragons loomed like large gargoyles on top. Selene's hand even gently brushed against his a couple of times.

"Remember," she said, slowing her pace as they approached another rectangular archway, "don't do anything unless I do something first."

"I won't," he nodded. Gawking up at the archway, forty feet tall and twenty feet wide, he noticed a great chair of stone in the distance. On either side, great urns burned with the glow of a purplish-red fire. He'd seen such thrones before, and the sight sent another sliver of ice through his scales.

A dragon, bronze and long necked, squawked above them. Other dragons squawked in return. It seemed their arrival had been announced.

"Let's go, then," Nath said. And through the archway they went.

CHAPTER

11

"WHAT IN GUZAN'S BEARD IS that?" Brenwar said, staring up into the sky.

Bayzog had returned with Samaz, but he'd kept Samaz's dream to himself. After all, dreams were open to interpretation.

"It looks like a rock," Ben said, craning his neck and shielding his eyes.

The sun was rising again, and Bayzog hadn't bothered to say anything until now. Everyone needed all the rest they could get, especially Sasha. Her pale eyes were bleary, and she stood by everyone else, gaping and yawning.

"How can this be, Bayzog?" she said. "It glows. Is it a dragon? A monster?"

Shum and Hoven crept along either side of her, staring as intently as everyone. Neither of the pair was ever rattled, so calm and poised in their expressionless demeanors. Now there was a puzzled, almost amazed look in their eyes. They glanced at each other and then at Bayzog.

Shum said, "Can you see it now, Bayzog?"

"It should seem familiar," Hoven added.

"Well, if you can see what it is, then why don't you spit it out?" Brenwar said, holding Pilpin by his ankles and up on his shoulders. "Does it kill the elves to be forthcoming about anything?"

"Why would that kill us?" Shum said.

Bayzog glided in between as Pilpin hopped off Brenwar's shoulders and bared his axes.

"A moment, everyone," Bayzog said, irritated, "if you please. We can wait, or I can shed some light upon this for all to see."

"Do it then, wizard," Brenwar said with a growl. "And make it quick. I'm about to pull the answers I want from a pair of elven skulls." He glared at Shum and Hoven. "That's no jest."

Bayzog spread his arms out wide, revealing his slender hands from the wide necks of his sleeves. His fingers drummed the morning air, and he started an incantation. Before his eyes, the air shimmered with new life. The distant view of the land and sky twisted and warbled. He summoned more power within and muttered the final word of the spell in Elven.

"*Ishpahlan*!"

Ben gasped the loudest of the group. Some of the others stepped back.

"By my beard, what have you done?" Pilpin said in wonderment.

"It's a wall of enhanced imagery," Bayzog said, "making everything appear much closer than it is."

"You can do that?"

"Fantastic, Father!" Rerry said, stepping closer to the wall. "Why haven't you shown me this before?" Everything was closer, ten times at least. The trees, the rocks, the birds that flew in the sky. Rerry stretched his hand out.

"Don't touch it!" Bayzog warned. "And don't stare so long, either. It'll make you dizzy."

Brenwar stood close by, clawing his beard and grumbling to himself. "Where'd that rock go?"

Bayzog narrowed his eyes. It took time to adjust to looking through the magic wall, but just when he saw it, Brenwar cried out.

"It's the Floating City!"

"That city?" Ben said, stepping closer. "Great Guzan! I see it now!"

The Floating City was there, floating straight toward them through the sky. Where it had seemed miles away, now it seemed as if it was right on top of them.

"Dragons are pulling that thing, Father," Rerry said. "Hundreds of them!"

There they were, shackled by enormous chains

to collars around their necks: dragons. All sorts. Black winged. Black tailed. All their eyes had a soft, green, radiant glow. Their leather wings labored over their backs as they pulled the city forward.

Bayzog felt Sasha's hand on his arm.

"Dearest," she said, "you have goose bumps. Never in my life have I ever seen you so stricken before."

"What do we do, Father?" Rerry said, drawing his sword. "What do we do?"

"I'll tell you what I'm going to do," Brenwar said. "I'm going to follow that city!"

CHAPTER

12

WHEN THE SQUAWKING OF VULTURES roused him, Gorlee's eyes fluttered open. He coughed, spat, and wiped the grit from the melted eyelets of his helmet. He rolled onto his back, wondering what was happening. A foul stench lingered in the air. He coughed again, louder this time, scattering the vultures that had landed.

How long have I been out?

He remembered the dragons. The intense heat. The screams. He had channeled his powers, changed, and blacked out, moments from his own flesh being charred to the bone. He pulled off the helmet he wore and studied the warped metal. The leather straps of his armor cracked and fell away. He peeled the remnants of metal from his stony skin and surveyed the area.

Oh my!

The human camp was smoke and ash now. Piles of bones and armor. Crawling on hands and knees, he looked around. Every man was dead. No survivors. The human ranks of Barnabus were gone.

So were the dragons, to his relief.

"What happened?" he gasped. "Why did they do this?" He staggered to his feet and stumbled through the ash. "Why did they leave so suddenly? I couldn't have been out that long, could I?"

Judging by the sun, it was nearing the end of the next day, or so he thought. But he wasn't sure. He broke off more of the stony cocoon that had formed over his skin, saving him from a certain end. Feeling weak and drained, he glanced at his pinkish skin.

"I'll need something thicker than that." He held his stomach and took a knee. "That dragon fire really sapped me." With the ghost of a new instinct born of playing Jason Haan for months, his hand fell to his waist and searched for his sword. He broke the brittle scabbard from the belt. The sword was gone. "Great. But when did I ever really need such a thing?"

Forcing himself up to his feet, he made his way through the camp. It seemed the army had taken a turn away from the path Selene and Nath had followed. He checked the sky.

No dragons. Good.

Heavy in thought and trying to figure out what was going on, he headed down the path Nath had taken.

I don't know what's happened, but I hope I'm not too late to aid Nath Dragon.

CHAPTER

13

PASSING UNDER THE HUGE STONE, Nath's senses caught fire. The landscape, the great throne, the colors of everything changed. He swore the sun rose and set. The moon emerged, dimmed, and made way for the sun to come out again. Holding his head, he squeezed his eyes shut and fought for his balance.

"What trick is this?" he said, reaching out for Selene. "Where are you?"

"I'm here," she said, clasping her arm in his. "Easy, Nath. The feeling will pass."

He pulled away and straightened himself. The moving ground seemed to settle beneath him. He glanced back at the monstrous portal. This side of it was still there, but changed somehow.

"Tell me," he said, "what is that?"

"A barrier in time. It can move you forward or

move you back. In this case," she said, tilting her head toward the sky. "It moved us forward."

As Nath looked up, every fiber of his being became taut. "Impossible!"

The Floating City hovered above. The jaxite stones, bright and brilliant blue, pulsated with eerie power.

"Isn't it magnificent?" Selene said, checking her nails. "It was one of my better ideas, actually. Using a few small stones only controlled a few dragons, but with the entire city of stone, well, I believe Gorn Grattack can control them all."

Nath gaped. This wasn't something he would have ever imagined. Control of the entire city's worth of powerful jaxite just might bend the will of all dragons who came near. Nalzambor wouldn't stand a chance.

"I thought we were in this together, Selene."

"Don't misunderstand me," she whispered, looking around. "I came up with this beforehand. I didn't expect it to bear fruit already, but seeing it now, well." She sighed. "It's exhilarating."

"You cannot control all of that power."

"No, Nath, you're right, I cannot."

Golden eyes as big as moons, Nath watched the dragons who rested on their perches atop the buildings in the city. They had great metal chains around their necks.

"Did they pull it here?" he said to Selene. His

blood became hot, and smoke rolled from his nostrils. "Was that your idea, too?"

"No, Nath Dragon," said a powerful, self-assured, bone-rattling voice. "It was mine."

Nath twisted his hips around and found himself facing the monstrous form of a dragon man.

"Allow me to introduce you to my master, Nath." Selene opened her palm out for display. "This ... is Gorn Grattack."

Nath felt his heart skip and then pound like thunder. This dragon man's evil aura disrupted every scale and every fiber of his makeup. Gorn stood eight feet in height, with great horns combed back from his head. His penetrating eyes burned with ice-cold fire. His countenance had hard, terrifying features. His scales shifted between white, grey, and black. His hands were great paws with steel-rending claws. Chin high and shoulders broad, there was an omnipotent air about him.

"Time to talk, Nath Dragon," Gorn said, turning his back on him. A great tail swept over the ground behind him as he headed toward the throne. "Come."

Nath had fought creatures far bigger than Gorn—giants, ettins, dragons, and the lurker—but he had never felt as small as he did now. Unlocking his frozen knees, he moved forward as if with a will not his own. The commanding power of Gorn's voice was overwhelming, much like that of his father, Balzurth.

Selene's firm but gentle touch pushed him along.

His eyes met hers.

They spoke to him through his muddled thoughts. *Don't do anything until I do.*

She had said that, but it might be too late to do anything by then. He'd have to trust her for now. He took a breath. Forced himself forward. He could handle being in the presence of his father, the most powerful dragon of all.

Certainly I can handle Gorn.

Blood rushed through him. His aversion to evil ignited over and over. His thoughts raced. What would become of Nalzambor under Gorn's rule? It would be devastated.

I must stop this monster! he thought, but the conviction was not there. *But how?*

Gorn stopped at the stone throne—which was still far too big for him—and turned.

"Can you feel it, Nath Dragon?" Gorn said. His tongue licked out, tasting the air.

"Feel what?"

"Defeat," Gorn said, hissing somewhat. "Inevitable defeat."

Nath pulled his shoulders back a little, lifted his chin, and said, "I'm surprised, Gorn. I thought you'd be more confident than that. I'm more than happy to accept your surrender." He looked at Selene, dusted his hands off, and added, "That was easy."

Gorn laughed a booming laugh. "Ha!" Flames shot from his nose. "I must admit, I've not done that in centuries. I give you credit, foolish gnat."

"It's Nath!"

Gorn's clawed hands clutched in and out. His black tongue licked over his snout. He then said, "I bet your father doesn't appreciate your clever tongue, but I find merit in it. The same as I do in a jackal when it laughs. Ha-ha-ha. Nath Dragon, Balzurth's lone spawn, born with a foul tongue. It's no surprise he is so disappointed in you."

"Everything can be disappointing. It just depends on your perspective of things. For example," Nath said, moving closer. "I'm disappointed in you. I expected you to be bigger. Scarier. But you're hardly a monster at all. I've seen worse." He glanced at Selene. "I've faced more terrible. Are you sure this is the Dark Dragon Lord?"

"Mind yourself, fool!" Selene said, drawing her hand back. "Silence your tongue!"

Nath couldn't. He tended to run his mouth when he was scared. It was a reflex of sorts. Something about his mouthing off soothed him within. Dropping his hands to his hips, he faced Gorn. "What do you want of me, Gorn? Do we fight? Talk? Bicker like old women at one another? Does my death give you victory in this war?"

"I don't need your death to win," Gorn said. "I won the moment you stepped through that portal. Ha-ha-ha."

Nath felt his scales stand up on end. What had happened? What had he done? "I don't see how."

"Oh," Gorn said, rubbing his chin, "you don't see it? Well then, let me show you." Gorn stretched his arms out toward the great stone portal and huffed in Dragonese. A brilliant mirage of dark colors twisted and turned within.

Slowly, images formed.

Nath turned and gaped.

Dragons covered the world in flame.

CHAPTER 14

T HERE IT WAS. DRAGONS. DEVASTATION. Towns
burned. People dead. Prisoners shackled.
Nath had to catch his breath. Never had he
imagined such horrors.

"How can this be?" he said in little more than
a whisper.

The dwarves marched from Morgdon. The
elves from Elome. The orcs of Thraag and their
horded army descended from the north. The image
in the great portal gave Nath glimpses of the entire
world. He'd watch long enough, enthralled, only
to see the image change into another. His blood
raced.

"What of the Truce?" he yelled a Selene. "You
knew of all this!"

"As I said," Gorn began, "the Truce, or rather,
the Lie, has ended. It ended before it even started."

Nath turned back to the portal. Dragons soared the skies, scraping the building tops with roaring flames gushing from their mouths. Towns he'd seen before were now cinders, the people dead, enslaved, or lost.

"What is the meaning of all this?" he said, turning and not holding back his anger. He clenched his fists, chest heaving. "Tell me why you do such wretched things!"

"I do this because dragons were meant to rule this world. Not men. Not elves. Not dwarves. Dragons!" Gorn said, stepping closer. He poked Nath in the shoulder, knocking him a step backward. "All will submit to me. Those who don't will perish. Especially your friends, Nath Dragon." He pointed at the grand mural. "Take a look. See."

He saw Brenwar wielding his war hammer and barking orders. Ben unleashed exploding arrows from Akron. Bayzog stood behind them, face in distress, arms shaking, shielding them and the others behind them. Dragons had them pinned down in the mountains, raining down blasts of fire upon them. They wouldn't last. They needed his help. Now. The image faded from one form to another. In Quintuklen, the city of humans, tall towers burned. The Legionnaires fought dragons and giants on the hillsides. Wave after wave of gnolls and goblins assaulted them.

Stretching his hand toward the portal, Nath

said, "Wait!" He needed to see what happened to Brenwar, Ben, and Bayzog.

"I've waited long enough," Gorn said with a sneer. "The end is what it is."

Nath's knees weakened. It wasn't supposed to be this way, was it? How had everything happened so fast? The portal must indeed have moved him through time. He needed to move it back. The image changed from one scene to another. He saw a blast of dragon fire shatter Bayzog's shield and drive Brenwar to his knees.

"Nooooo!" Nath yelled. He gathered his legs and sprang through the portal. The image faded, and he fell face first on the ground. Spitting the dirt out of his mouth, he glared back at Gorn and Selene.

Gorn was laughing. "Fool!" the dragon warlord said, crossing his arms over his chest. "A fool indeed. Perhaps this fool would like to make a bargain."

Nath came to his feet. "I don't bargain with evil."

"Is that so?" Gorn lifted a scaly brow. "Even if it could save your friends? Save most of the world, perhaps?"

"No."

"I think you should at least look and see what I have to offer, Nath." Gorn turned and started to walk away, and Selene followed. "Come."

Eyeing the dragons perched on the stones above, Nath followed after them with a heavy heart. His friends were in danger. Possibly dying. And all he was doing was nothing.

This can't be happening. It can't be!

Above, he heard a rattle of chains. He stopped to look. The dragons tethered to the Floating City took flight. With great effort in their wings and angry growls coming from their throats, they began pulling at the chains tethered to the city. Slowly, inch by inch, foot by foot, the city began to spin clockwise.

Sultans of Sulfur! What are they doing?

He followed Gorn and Selene behind the great stone throne. Ahead, Gorn had stopped. His broad, muscular, scale-ridged back blocked the view of something that captured his attention. Selene stood at the monster's side, tail sliding side to side in unison with Gorn's. She seemed insignificant beside him. It reminded him of how Nath felt ofttimes when he stood beside his father.

Could he be her father? That would explain a lot.

If that were the case, his cause might be lost already. Nath proceeded, coming to a stop beside Selene, where a large altar of stone sat on the brown and dusty ground. A dragon was chained down on the bloodstained slab. A gold one.

"You dare!" Nath said. He jumped up on top

of the dais and tugged at the moorite chains, straining.

The dragon's eyes fluttered open. She had long lashes and beautiful pink- and gold-flecked eyes. She moaned, soft and miserable.

"Release her!"

"No," Gorn said, slowly shaking the great horns on his head. "I cannot do that. But you can, Nath Dragon. You can release her from this life that offers only a horrible end." Gorn reached over and grabbed a great spear that was stuck in the ground. It was eight feet in length and had a large, barbed head and a razor-sharp tip. "Her life for your friends' lives."

Still tugging at the unbreakable links, Nath groaned, "Aaarererer!" and his brow beaded with sweat. "I don't do your evil deeds!" he said through clenched teeth. "Not now! Not ever!"

Gorn eyed the spear tip. "Please. Settle yourself. You're in no condition to break those chains." He thumbed the edge. "Sharp. Now Nath, do you know the best way to kill a dragon? After all, we have scales, harder than steel. Armor all over. We are fast, but we can still be defeated. What is it that kills us so well?"

Nath didn't answer. Instead, he eased his efforts and rubbed the dragon's head. She snorted a little. Selene had already tried to fool him into killing one dragon, a rose blossom, before. Why would they tempt him now and try to make him kill a magnificent golden-tailed lady, the sweetest and gentlest of all the dragon breeds, if not the rarest as well?

"The heart," Gorn continued. "One swift, hard strike will do it. But not with just anything. It takes magic steel, or an enchanted dragon part, such as a horn. That is what this fine tip is crafted from, the horn of a steel dragon. I think you knew this one once."

Nath sneered. All he could think of was the one he had met guarding the tombs in the Shale Hills. That dragon was a powerful one. More powerful than inferno, maybe.

"Take it," Gorn said. "Better her life be lost to a friend than to my kind." Somehow, the dragon warlord smiled. "Consider it mercy, far better treatment than what I have in store for your friends."

A lump formed in Nath's throat. He glanced at Selene.

There was a glimmer of sympathy in her dark eyes.

"I'm not feeling very patient, Nath Dragon." He held the spear out toward Nath. "Her life for your friends' lives. You must decide now."

CHAPTER

15

"HOLD ON! HOLD ON!" SASHA yelled. She'd locked her hands around Bayzog's waist and now began feeding him power. "I'm with you!"

They'd followed the Floating City for three days, trying to keep up as it moved swiftly beneath the clouds. The dragons that hauled it along had paid them so little mind that for a long time, Bayzog had no reason to believe they even saw them. Then they had struck.

Huddled inside a small ravine in the hills, Bayzog secured them with his shield. It had begun to crack under the blistering heat. Dragons dove from the air, blasting fire one right after the other.

"We have to find a way out of here," Brenwar yelled. "Pilpin, find us a hole!" The grizzled dwarf wound up his war hammer. Beside him, Ben reloaded his bow. "Let them have it!" He released the hammer. Ben shot his bow.

The war hammer shattered the teeth of a diving grey scaler.

Crack!

An exploding arrow busted the wing of another.

Boom!

Both dragons spun out of control and slammed into the rocky slopes of the mountain.

"For Morgdon, lizards!"

Another series of flames danced and sizzled on Bayzog's shield. Gripping the Elderwood Staff with all his might, he summoned more power. The cracks in the shield strengthened. Above, in the nooks in the rock, Shum and Hoven went to work with their Dragon Needles, jabbing at anything that came close enough to attack, keeping some of the smaller crawling dragons at bay.

"Father," Rerry said, brandishing his sword, "let me fight!"

"No, Son! Stay back."

"But—"

"I said *no*."

"Brenwar," Ben said, firing another shot, "what about your hammer?"

"Guzan!" Brenwar yelled. He dashed away and disappeared over the edge of the ravine.

"Get back here!" Ben yelled. "You'll get

slaughtered out there!" He looked back at Bayzog. "I have to go after him."

"Don't," Bayzog said, starting his argument, but Ben was already dashing out of the ravine. Rerry followed, lithe as a gazelle. "Rerry, come back!"

"Rerry!" Sasha screamed after her son. "No!" She released Bayzog, stumbled over the loose stones in the ravine, and fell. Pain erupted in her face.

"Sasha!" Bayzog said, reaching out for her.

A roar of flame coated the shield. The bright-orange, blistering flames blinded his eyes. A bolt of lightning lanced through the shield, and again it began to crack.

Ssszram!

Another bright blast came, shattering the shield into shards and knocking Bayzog from his feet. Numb and shaking, he rolled off his back and tried to gather his feet. Strong hands hoisted him up. He looked back and saw Samaz.

"Look!" Samaz said with wide fear-filled eyes. "Mother!"

Twenty feet away, Sasha was hemmed in by a pair of dragons, a blue streak and a grey scaler, each standing one head taller than Sasha. Tongues licked from their mouths, and angry hisses came forth.

Brow buckled, Bayzog unleashed power from the Elderwood Staff.

Kra-Cow!

A blinding bolt of intense golden power erupted from the staff, incinerating the grey scaler. The blue streak darted away.

Bayzog and Samaz rushed over to Sasha and helped her stand. Her robes were torn, and one knee was bleeding.

"Are you all right?"

"Yes," she said, dusting off her robes. "I should have been able to handle that. What a fool I am. I had a spell on my lips and could not—"

A great shadow filled the ravine, and all parties looked up. A huge sky raider descended, its great jaws wide open. In an instant, Bayzog finally realized his shield was gone. The scales on the beast's chest became bright like flame, and it blasted the ravine with an ear-splitting roar. Covering his ears, Bayzog fell to his knees. Sasha was shaking, and the heat alone from the great dragon's breath was suffocating. A snort of flame shot from its nose, and the blackness of its massive maw began to glow.

"Do something, Father!" Samaz said.

Bayzog's thoughts went blank.

"Did you find it?" Ben said to Brenwar, bow ready, eyeing the sky.

"No," Brenwar yelled, ripping a small tree out of the earth.

A dragon burst from the foliage, little bigger than him. Its mouth filled with flames that began to gush out.

Brenwar stuffed the small tree into its mouth. "Chew on that, fire breather!"

A copper dragon head emerged from the woodland and dashed into the clearing. Its tail swiped the ground and lifted Brenwar from his feet.

Brenwar's head cracked a rock. "I've had enough of you lizards!" He snatched up the rock his head had broken and hurled it at the dragon.

The monster slithered aside and pounced on Brenwar. Claws tore at his eyes and limbs. Its tail curled around his throat.

"Now yer making me mad," Brenwar spat at the beast. He cocked back his arm and punched it with all the power of his bracer.

Whop! Whop! Whop!

The dragon hissed. Acid flames dripped from its mouth, but the stubborn monster held on, dripping acid onto Brenwar's armor so that it sizzled and burned holes in his now-smoking beard.

"Now you've done it!"

Whop whop whop!
Whop whop whop!

The dragon's ribs cracked, making tree-like splintering sounds.

Cri-crick crick!

Its body softened and wavered. Its tail went slack around his neck.

Brenwar grabbed its tail and slung the two-hundred-pound dragon like a man slinging a cat.

It crashed into a tree and moved no more.

Nearby, Ben loosed another arrow into a dragon's neck, dropping it from the sky. The warrior locked eyes with him and nocked another arrow.

"Brenwar, look out!"

Out of nowhere, a grey scaler pounced on his back, driving him face first to the ground.

"Blasted lizards!" Fighting to regain his footing and ignoring the clawing at his back, Brenwar twisted over. He shoved the limp form of the dragon off him. "What happened?" he said. "I didn't even hit it." And then he noticed Rerry.

The young part-elf warrior brushed his light hair from his eyes, staring at the blood on his sword. "I—I killed it," Rerry said, staring down at the dragon. "With my sword."

Brenwar got up on his feet. "You did well, part of a part-elf. Now stop gawking and help me find my hammer." His eyes scoured the landscape. "Ah, there it is." Making his way toward the brush, he stopped and picked up his war hammer.

Above, a great dragon blotted out the light of

the sun and landed over the ravine. Another one circled over the first.

"Sultans of Sulfur," Ben said. "Not another one."

"We have to get back," Rerry said, "Mother and Father are up there!"

CHAPTER 16

A STORM BREWED INSIDE NATH DRAGON. The mere idea of shedding innocent blood infuriated him. After all, he was the one destined to protect the dragons from such horrific things. Now Gorn and Selene had tried in a more subtle way to get him to kill an innocent dragon, a female. It was madness. Why would he ever do such a thing?

He looked the dragon in the eye and petted her snout. She wasn't young, but perhaps the same age as him. Bright scaled and beautiful. A beautiful vision most people only dreamed of seeing.

"I'll save you," he softly said under his breath. "Somehow." He closed his eyes and thought of his friends. They were dying out there, all because of him. Gorn offered to save them if he killed this one dragon. And then what? His thoughts raced.

Think it through, Dragon. Think it through.

"Time is up, Nath Dragon," Gorn said. "And I'm certain your dear friends' lives hang by a thread. Seconds remain, maybe."

Lies!

Evil always lies.

Perhaps, Nath thought, *everything I've seen is a lie. Why should I do anything Gorn says? Or Selene, for that matter?* His mind turned it over in those moments. What of his friends, who he feared he'd never see again? They'd made it clear to him before that they were ready to die for him. He had never understood what that meant until right now.

He turned and faced Gorn Grattack. Stepping forward, he grabbed Gorn's spear by the tip and held it to his chest.

Gorn leered down at him, brow lifted.

"You win, Gorn. But I offer you something better. My life for hers and the lives of my friends. I need your word on that."

"What?" Selene said, coming forward, hands balled up into fists. "Don't be a fool, Nath!"

"Back away, Selene!" Gorn said, sneering at her. "You disappoint me!" Gorn pulled the spear away from Nath and rested it on his shoulder. Glowering at Nath with blazing eyes, he said, "You disappoint me as well."

"My father, Balzurth, didn't raise me to kill dragons. He raised me to save them." He swallowed.

He could feel something swelling inside his chest. A wonderful epiphany of sorts. "I understand that now."

"What sort of fool would die for those who don't even care about him? All your life, have the dragons not rejected you?"

"I'm over it," Nath said, stepping forward and taking a knee with a newfound inner strength. "If I have to die for them, then so be it."

"Nath, don't!" Selene said.

"Silence!" Gorn said, in more of a roar than a word. His rumbling voice shook the ground. "Nath Dragon, do you know what a pawn is?"

"Of course I do," Nath said, looking up at Gorn's terrifying face. "And I suppose you're going to tell me I've been a pawn all along. A tool of my father's. Even so, I stand by my word and his words. If it's his will for me to be his pawn, then so be it. I believe in him."

Gorn sneered and tossed back his head and let out a frightening roar.

Nath wasn't sure if Gorn felt angry or triumphant.

Above, the Floating City continued to spin around and around, getting faster and faster.

"Your father has his pawn," Gorn said. "And I have mine. The jaxite combined with my power will bring even more dragons under my control. Once I have them, I'll take over your father's precious Dragon Home and make it once again my Mountain of Doom."

"Not without a fight."

"He won't put up much of a fight after you're gone, let me assure you." Gorn bounced the spear off his shoulder. "Huh," he said, snorting smoke, "part of me wants to thank you, but I don't thank anyone." He started to lower the spear. "And I've waited long enough for this."

Nath lifted his chin and closed his eyes. He heard his heartbeat in his ears and felt Gorn poised to strike. He didn't flinch when the spear sliced through the air.

Glitch!

He heard the tip pierce through scales, separating bone and marrow. He didn't feel a thing.

A soft, painful moan caught Nath's ears.

His eyes snapped open, and he screamed.

"Selene!"

CHAPTER 17

AFTER THE SLAUGHTER, GORLEE HAD scraped up fragments of armor, strapped them on, and taken on the form of a lizard man. He'd pushed though the heavy brush of the hillside, avoiding the path Selene and Nath had taken. Wingless dragons patrolled the path along the harsh woodland, escorted by draykis. He'd already had enough close calls the past few days. He'd gotten close, only to be pushed back again. His thick lizard hide saved him aggravation when hiding in the thorns and thistles.

Why do I have the feeling I'll not get within a mile of Nath Dragon?

He kept hoping a human patrol or squad of the army would come down the path, but it didn't happen. It was just draykis and dragons, not to mention the fiery eyes that peered down at him.

The valley he sought to invade was a well-fortified hole.

Through the trees, he eyed two armored draykis leading a pair of six-legged blue dragons the size of ponies. The dragons snorted at the path, sniffing the leaves on the trees and growling.

Gorlee hunkered down deep into the brush. His heart started pounding. He'd been evading the dragons for days, but he couldn't keep it up much longer. They knew he was near. They'd figure him out.

Be still. Don't take any chances.

"Come on," a draykis said, tugging on the chain that held the dragon by a heavy collar on its neck. "All you're doing is sniffing branches." He jerked the chain.

The dragon blasted fire at his feet.

The draykis hopped over the flame toward the dragon and swatted its horned head.

Whop!

"Don't do that again!"

The dragon's throat rumbled, but its neck bent down. Slowly, it turned and headed back down the path. The other draykis and dragon followed.

Gorlee gave it a few minutes and let out a breath.

Whew!

Once again, he pushed through the thickets and came to a stop on a crag that overlooked a crescent moon–shaped valley. It was distant, but among the treetops he could make out great stones standing tall in the valley. At least a dozen dragons were perched on those rocks, and more were coming. They glided in and landed while others departed and disappeared. But that wasn't what enamored Gorlee at the moment.

I never would have believed it if I wasn't seeing it for myself.

The Floating City hovered above, with the jaxite stones twinkling and throbbing with life. Nath Dragon had caught him up on a few things, and the Floating City this had to be. He also recalled the undead army that waited inside, and he started to count all the dragons perched on the building tops. There must have been at least a hundred that he could see, and others that weren't tethered by chains were still flying in and out. A chill went through him.

What kind of army can stand against such a fortress?

Ignoring the trepidation within, he renewed his descent to the bottom of the mountain and the crescent-moon valley below.

I don't know if Nath Dragon needs me, or if I need him.

Gorlee had made it another hundred yards or so when a loud commotion cut through the trees. It sounded like a fire and a skirmish of sorts. He swore his keen ears heard a woman cry out. He shook his head.

It's a trap. It must be.

Nath had told him how some dragons played games when they baited their prey. He needed to be careful when he heard strange calls that cried out through the darkness. He glanced down the hill. He was getting closer to his goal, and he felt drawn to those great stones, but the sounds he heard were too tempting. Trusting his instincts, he rushed off toward the sound of danger.

Heroes do stupid things like this all the time.

He hopped a fallen tree, sped down into a clearing, and surged toward the other side.

Ssslap! Ssslap!

Dragon tails hanging like vines from the branches knocked him onto his backside. Two forest-green-scaled dragons plopped to the ground, heads low and hissing. In an instant, they had scrambled over the ground, and fierce jaws seized him by the leg and arm.

Gorlee screamed. The pain was blinding.

Change form! Change form!

The jaws of the black-tailed emerald dragons locked, and like angry bulldogs they tried to tug him apart.

"Nooooo!"

CHAPTER 18

BLANK. BAYZOG, WHO PRIDED HIMSELF on being prepared for anything great or small, was dumbstruck.

"Father!" Samaz said again.

Eyes filled with destruction, the sky-raider dragon's chest glowed with new light. Flames shot out of its nose.

Screaming, "Give me that!" Sasha snatched the Elderwood Staff from his grip and held it out before them.

The ancient piece of polished wood glowed with an intense, brilliant white light.

The dragon roared and recoiled.

"Be gone, monster!" Sasha yelled as the staff's light became brighter and brighter.

Samaz rushed alongside his mother and yelled as well. "Go!"

The dragon turned its neck and shielded its eyes with its wing, letting out an awful-sounding roar that shook the mountain.

Bayzog shook his head, blinking. *What am I doing?*

Suddenly, the radiant light winked out, and he heard Sasha say, "Oh no!" She didn't have control over the staff, but she'd had just enough to distract the dragon.

Baring its claws, it turned on them again with a nasty angry growl.

They were still cornered.

Gathering his wits, he bounded over and grabbed the staff.

"I'm sorry, Bayzog," Sasha said, "I tried."

"You did well! Now get behind me and hold on to me and the staff. Both of you!"

As the dragon started to let loose its breath, Bayzog felt power surge through him like never before. The wills of Sasha and Samaz forged a desperate bond with his and let loose a cannon of power.

Sssrazz-Booom!

A blast of blue-white energy punched a whole clean through the dragon and sent it spinning in the air. It flopped in midair and tumbled crashing through the trees, toppling timbers and pines in its death throes. Its ear-splitting howl was knee bending.

Bayzog took a deep breath and let both his own power and that of the staff fill him. He'd been holding back for years, decades even, but he couldn't hold back now. This was it.

"Stay close," he said to his family, "And thank you. Your bravery saved us."

"We are here to help," Sasha said, catching her breath, "I'm more than a lovely face, you know."

"Father," Samaz yelled, pointing toward the sky. "Another dragon comes!"

"Kill that dragon!" Brenwar yelled, winding up his hammer. "I've had my fill of them!"

Just as he finished saying it, a bolt of power ripped through the back of the sky raider that landed, sending it hurtling through the trees.

The second dragon sailed downward in its place, its claws and fangs bared.

Twang!

An exploding arrow rocketed through the air and hit the dragon underneath its wings, which sent it spinning out of control.

"Good shot," Rerry said, "but we need to finish it."

Ben and Rerry darted ahead and sprinted for the ravine. Legs churning, Brenwar huffed along behind them, dragging Pilpin along with him. He glanced above and noted that the skies were clear. Only the Floating City remained behind them, and it had dragons whizzing out of it and draped all over it. He clambered up the hill as fast as his stout legs would take him, following the busted trees in the forest.

"Where'd you go?"

Crack!

Out of nowhere, a tail whipped out and sent both Brenwar and Pilpin spinning head over heels. He pushed his face out of the dirt and shook his beard. Head low, a grey scaler crept in with its tongue slithering out of its mouth.

Brenwar swung and missed.

Whoosh!

Pilpin was going in when a bolt of lightning shot from the dragon's mouth and hit Brenwar square in his chest plate.

Zap!

Every hair stood up on end, and he staggered back into the trees with a painful tingling from head to toe. He shook his head like an angry bull and said, "Now you've made me mad!"

The dragon darted in at full speed, knocking Pilpin clean away with its tail.

"Aaaaahhhhhhhhhh!" Pilpin cried as he sailed over the trees.

Timing it, Brenwar brought War Hammer around with all his power. A thunder clap followed.

Ka-Pow!

A dragon horn shattered, and the beast sagged to the ground.

Still tingling, Brenwar forged ahead.

The sky raider, ten tons of scales and towering twenty feet high, fought everything coming. Shum and Hoven darted in and out with their Dragon Needles. Ben volleyed arrow after arrow, and Rerry taunted the beast.

Mad and confused, the dragon struck. Its claws tore up the ground as it pounced after Rerry.

"Eep!" Rerry said, springing away from the snapping jaws of the dragon at the last second.

Shum knifed inside and jammed a Dragon Needle in its eye.

The dragon reared up with a roar, and a blast of yellow flames shot out of its mouth. In a flash, its great tail swept over the ground.

Ben and Rerry moved, but not fast enough. The tail swept them aside and flung them across the ground. Both man and part elf lay still and broken.

"No!" Brenwar yelled, charging straight for the dragon's belly. Speeding underneath its swinging tail, he smashed it in the belly. Ancient metal powered by magic bracers met ancient scale.

Krang-Boom!

Scales shattered. Bones splintered. The dragon staggered backward on its haunches and fell.

Hoven, like a shadow, moved in and struck.

Glitch!

He pierced the dragon's chest, straight into its heart.

The beast huffed one last breath of fire, and its glowing eyes went out as it died.

"Ben! Rerry!" Brenwar rushed over to them. They were breathing. "Wake up!"

"Perhaps a gentler approach," Shum said, strolling over.

Brenwar shoved him away and kneeled down to pinch Ben.

Ben's eyes snapped open. "Ow!" The warrior started to his feet. "Ow!"

"I didn't even touch you that time," Brenwar said.

Ben winced. "I think my arm is broken."

"Well, you should have been paying better attention," Brenwar said. "Ducked, jumped, or something."

"Not everyone is made out of stone like you dwarves."

"Oh!" Rerry said, as Shum and Hoven jostled him up, "and I think my leg is broken."

Brenwar shook his head. "Great, just great. Now I'm going to have to carry the both of you."

"You aren't carrying me," said Ben, "My legs are just fine."

A branch cracked from somewhere nearby. Everyone's stance became battle ready. Shum and

Hoven crept forward and spread out wide just as a figure emerged.

It was Pilpin. "Save any dragon for me?" he said, lifting his brow.

"Did you find us a cave yet?" Brenwar said.

"No, did you?"

"Pah!"

A moment later, Bayzog, Sasha, and Samaz emerged from the brush.

"Rerry!" Sasha said, rushing over to his side.

"I'll be fine, Mother. I'm just glad you and Father are well." He looked at his brother, who had the faintest smile on his grim face. "Even Samaz."

Change form! Change form!

Gorlee could feel the emerald dragons biting down into his flesh, sinking their teeth in deeper and deeper. He screamed. "Ee-yah!"

One tugged on his arm and the other pulled on his leg, stretching his body taut as a bowstring.

Come on, change, Gorlee!

It was hard to concentrate and fight the blinding pain at the same time. All his life, he'd been clever enough to avoid such unpleasant circumstances. But today, this very minute, it had all caught up with him.

They're going to eat me! Guzan, no!

95

He squeezed his eyes shut, blocked out the pain, and thought of the hardest thing that he knew. He saw the great stones in the valley, and his skin began turning to living stone. His pain faded, and his strength renewed. With his free arm, he punched one of the dragons in the head. Its jaws loosened, and it recoiled with a hiss. He grabbed the other one by the horns and twisted its neck until it released his arm. Its claws raked at his stony skin. Gorlee flung it away.

"Be gone, lizards!"

With leery eyes and tongues flickering from their mouths, the dragons flanked him. Their black tails slithered from side to side.

Gorlee kicked at them. "Go away if you know what's good for you!"

Together, the dragons opened their mouths and spat out blasts of bright-green fire. The flames engulfed Gorlee from head to toe.

"Argh!"

His stony skin was tough, but nothing was completely resistant to dragon fire. The suffocating heat dropped him to his knees, and he curled up into a ball. His stone-hard skin sizzled.

Hang on, Gorlee! They can't breathe out forever! Hang on!

The roar of fire filled his ears. Every second felt like ten. The heat was excruciating. Unbearable. He felt faint and dizzy. He tried to concentrate on something else, anything else, but he couldn't focus.

I'm not going to make it.

Whoosh!

The flames stopped. The air felt ice cold on his smoking skin. He opened his eyes and started to rise.

"Stay still, lizard man," a voice said. It was familiar, dwarven.

Two tall elven men with pot bellies stood over the emerald dragons with spears driven into them. The dragons were dead, and the dwarf who spoke was ...

"Brenwar?"

"What kind of lizard man are you?" Brenwar said.

Another dwarf, much smaller than Brenwar, rushed in and chopped his axe into Gorlee's leg. The blade skipped off.

"This lizard man is a living statue," Pilpin said. He swung his axe into the back of Gorlee's legs this time, sweeping him off his feet. "A fallen statue."

Suddenly, Gorlee was hemmed in with spear tips and axe blades.

One of the elven men spoke, pointing a spear tip at his neck, saying, "This will penetrate anything."

Brenwar jostled his axe over him, saying, "And this will do much worse than what this elf thinks he can do."

Gorlee swallowed hard. His friends weren't toying with him. And judging by the hard looks in their battle-scarred faces, he'd better be careful how he chose his next words. Slowly, he held up his palms, closed his eyes, turned his cheek and said, "I'm Gorlee. Please don't kill me, friends?"

CHAPTER 19

"**Y**OU SAY HE'S DOWN THERE?" Bayzog said. He stood on an overlook, hidden by the trees. All the others were there except Ben, Sasha, and Rerry. She was treating the wounded. "The Half Moon Valley of Stones. Interesting."

"What's so interesting about it?" Brenwar said, looking through a spyglass. "Just roughhewn stones."

"They're portals."

"To where?"

Bayzog ignored him. He was more interested in what Gorlee, who stood beside him in the form of a large roughhewn stone himself, had to say. He stared at the changeling.

"What? Better than a goblin—or a dwarf," Gorlee said to Brenwar.

"Hah!"

"Perhaps you'd prefer an orc," Gorlee said. "I expected you'd be glad to see me."

"Glad ... har, never!"

"It's not your appearance," Bayzog said, "it's your story. Nath Dragon and Selene. Why would he do such a thing?"

Gorlee had already told them about his abduction and Selene's betrayal, but he still didn't understand Nath's motivation.

"I guess Nath needed to see what he was up against."

"You should have stopped him," Brenwar said.

"And blown my cover? I couldn't do that. They'd have killed us all, not that they didn't try once already." Gorlee towered over Brenwar with his hands on his hips. "Hundreds of men died just after he left."

"Back up, changeling, or whatever you are." Brenwar poked at him with the war hammer. "I'm not going to mourn men who served on the side of evil. Now, get out of my way. I'm going down there and dragging him out myself."

"There's scores of dragons down there," Bayzog said, stepping in his way. "Not to mention the hundreds that watch from above in the city. Set your frustration and anger aside. Let's think about this. At least we know Nath is close, and I'm grateful for that."

"Hrmph!"

"We need a plan," Shum said, stepping in. "But I fear we might be too late."

"Why do you say that?" Brenwar said.

Shum pointed toward the Floating City. The jaxite glowed with new life, and the dragons tethered to the chains were flying again, with their great wings beating. Slowly, the city began to turn in the sky. Little by little, it picked up speed.

Eyes tilted upward, Bayzog said, "I have a bad feeling about this."

"What do you mean?" Brenwar said. "Spit it out, elf."

"If I were to guess ... that city and all that stone, it's a beacon."

"A beacon for what?"

"A beacon that will not only attract but control more dragons."

"And how many of those do you think it will control?" Gorlee said.

"With that much jaxite? I'd say all of them."

Brenwar stormed away, found his chest, and picked it up by the outside handles. He headed back to the rest of the party and dropped it at their feet. They all stared.

"What are you looking at me like that for?"

"What do you propose we do with that," Shum said, eyeing it, "put our boots in it?"

Hoven laughed.

"Brenwar," Bayzog said, kneeling down and opening the chest up wide. "I understand what you're thinking, but even this and all the powers stored within, I don't think it will help us enough."

"Nath went in there with nothing at all, as I understand it. At least we have this. Now is the time to help him." Brenwar looked into the darkening sky. Lightning streaked across it, and more dragons flew into the city. "Now is the time. I feel it in these bones of mine."

Bayzog fingered the items in the chest. There were rows of potions in small, bright vials, ornate tokens and objects, strangely woven cloths, wands, orbs, tools, and stones of many colors. He plucked a yellow vial from the shelf and tossed it to Hoven.

"Take that to Sasha and tell her to use it on Ben and Rerry, if you please."

Hoven started to slide away, but Ben's strong voice stopped him.

"I'll take it from here," he said, coming closer and looking into the chest. His arm was in a sling, and his bearded face was scratched up something fierce. "I think what you have in there can certainly help us, but this is what Dragon needs."

Ben held out Fang, who was still sheathed in his scabbard. The dragonhead hilt's tiny gemstone eyes were glowing, and puffs of smoke flared from their nostrils. "Fang's trying to talk to me. I think he misses Dragon."

Eyes resting on Fang's hilt, the wizard's face brightened a little. He was certain Nath was alive. The possible futures shown in Samaz's dreams didn't always come to pass. It was clear to Bayzog, inside his gut, that Nath still lived. He'd been hesitant before to let his friends rush in, fearing the venture might be futile, that Nath was gone. For now, this was not the case. There was still time to help their lost friend.

"That settles it, then," Brenwar said, standing tall and picking up his war hammer, "we're going down there now."

And then the ground shook. Stones cracked. A gut-wrenching dragon bellow rose up out of the valley and swayed the trees and timbers.

"BAH-ROOOOOOOO!"

"What in Guzan's beard was that?" Brenwar said.

Another thunderous dragon cry rose up. Dragon flames blasted into the sky down from the valley.

"*What* was it?" Bayzog said, unable to hide his bewilderment. "'*Who* was it' is more like it..." All of his fears came to life. "I don't know why, but I'm certain that was—"

Brenwar stepped out on the overlook and finished his sentence.

"Nath Dragon."

CHAPTER 20

"SELENE!" NATH CRIED.

Gorn ripped the spear out of her chest. "Fool of a traitor!"

Nath caught her as she teetered backward, gasping, and fell into his arms.

"Why, Selene, why?"

Her dark eyes were spacey as she touched his cheek. "Because you are the only one who can stop him, Nath." She coughed and spat a little blood. "Only you can." Her tail snaked around his shoulder and stroked his mane of hair. "And because"—*cough-cough*—"I..."

Her tail slipped off his shoulders. Her eyes turned glassy. Selene was gone.

Tears swelled in Nath's eyes as his thoughts raced and he tried to make sense of it all. "Nooooooooo!" he yelled at the top of his lungs. "Nooooooooo!"

His bloodshot eyes locked on Gorn, who stood nearby leaning on the bloody spear.

There was a smile on the dragon warlord's face. "She was a pawn, nothing more. Her weakness was her end." He flashed a face filled with razor-sharp teeth. "I see you share the same weakness as hers." He shrugged. "Oh well, it seems now I have to finish this." He flicked up the spear. In a snap, he flung it at Nath Dragon.

Nath shifted his shoulders and snatched the spear out of the air. "No! Now it's your time to die, Gorn! I'm going to make you pay. For this, and for everything else you've done!" He lowered the spear point. In a blur of motion, he charged.

The spear plunged through Gorn's chest with ram-like force, pinning his back against the rock.

Gorn groaned, and then suddenly he started to laugh. Loud and thunderous. "Ha! Ha! Ha! Ha!"

Slap!

Gorn's backhand sent Nath flying through the air.

After crashing into the throne, Nath scurried to his feet. His chest was heaving.

Gorn pulled the spear out of his body and flung it aside. "No stick can kill me, boy. Nothing can kill a heartless dragon."

Nath glanced at Selene's broken body. She was dead. It was impossible to believe. Eyeing Gorn, all he could do was scream at the top of his lungs, "BAH-ROOOOOOOO!"

His dragon heart charged. His dragon blood pumped like never before. His scales popped and rippled. Gorn, the stones, and Selene started shrinking. Power filled him. Awesome power that he had never felt before. At least not since that time he flew with Selene.

Gorn cocked his horned head and stared at him with suspicion. Then he glanced down at Selene with anger in his eyes. "Traitor of a daughter! You did this! You let the poison wear off!" He dipped his chin. "So be it, then."

Nath's enraged thoughts clicked into place. The food she fed him. It stifled his powers and his ability to change into a dragon. Selene had always fussed about him not eating enough, and now he understood why. But these last few days, she hadn't made him eat.

Gorn clenched his fists at his sides. His horns charged up with power. He grew and transformed, from a huge draykis-like being to a full-sized dragon and then some. He had gigantic arms, powerful legs, and a beastly and ancient smile. He let out a roar the sound of a hundred dragons in one.

" B A H - R H O O O O O O O O - THAAAAAAAAAAAAA!"

It shook the valley.

Nath Dragon, still growing, let out a thunderous

roar of his own. "BAH-RHOOOOOOOOO-THAA!" Nath charged.

The dragon titans, each thirty feet tall, collided. *BOOM!*

Gorn's tail caught Nath behind the neck and jerked him down to the ground. A bright blast of deep-purple power shot from his mouth, pounding into Nath. It sent him skidding across the ground and back into the throne. Bright, painful spots formed in his eyes.

"Stay down, foolish Nath!" Gorn said, lording it over him. "You might have a dragon's body now, but you have no experience in how to use it. Let me teach you."

Nath shook his head and started up on his feet. He glared at Gorn. "Teach me? Hah! I'll teach you!" His chest charged up in brilliant yellow light. He unleashed the fury within. Dragon fire blasted from his mouth, slamming Gorn in the chest.

The dragon warlord teetered backward, covering his face, and fell.

Nath pounced. Landing on Gorn, he started punching with all his might. He landed one earth-shaking punch after the other.

Gorn flailed wildly and tried to scurry away, but Nath held him down and kept hammering.

Whop! Whop! Smack! Smack! Smack!

Gorn groaned. His bright-yellow eyes became wild with fear. "Yield! I yield, Nath Dragon!"

Nath paused. His dragon chest was heaving. He started to speak, changed his mind, and started to hit.

Wham! Wham! Wham!

"Please stop!" Gorn cried out. "Please stop!"

Nath held back.

"Your powers, Nath, I underestimated them. You have more mastery than I imagined." Gorn's yellow eyes turned bright as the sun. "But not more mastery than me!"

Beams of power blasted from Gorn's eyes.

Nath jerked away a split second too late.

The blast ripped through his shoulder and sent him backward.

Holding his burning shoulder, Nath forced himself up to one knee.

"Dragons," Gorn ordered to the sky, "Kill the prince. Kill Nath Dragon!"

The dragons who were patiently waiting perched on the stones spread their wings and attacked.

One of the stone portals flared with a strange swirl of mystic life nearby.

Gorn dashed through it and disappeared.

Nath raced after him, stopping short as a hull dragon, dark purple, launched itself out of the portal.

The two collided with a thunderous crash and became an angry knot of scales battling for their lives on the ground.

CHAPTER

21

I N HIS DRAGON FORM, NATH smashed his clawed fist into the hull dragon, rocking its head backward.

It regained its balance and unleashed the churning forces of its powerful breath.

Nath ducked under the searing heat and tackled it. It was bigger and slower, and Nath's superior speed and claws tore into it.

It howled in pain and fury.

Nath howled back. Angry now, he clutched its neck, pinned it down, and unleashed the fires within. The flames engulfed the hull dragon's face.

It writhed and twisted, but Nath held it fast, letting his flames do the work until the monster moved no more. Nothing but a searing, smoking skull remained when Nath stood up and pounded its face in triumph.

The celebration was cut short.

Sa-Boom! Sa-Boom! Sa-Boom!

Fireballs, lightning, acid bombs, and mystic needles assaulted him from above, where dragons filled the air, circling and diving: sky raiders, grey scalers, bull dragons, blue streaks... One right after the other, they dove and nipped, unleashing breath weapons from their mouths.

The furious assault overwhelmed Nath and dropped him to his knees. He covered up with his arms.

There must be a hundred up there!

A bull dragon flew straight into him, knocking him over. Grey scalers latched onto his legs with their teeth. Fireball after lightning bolt and lightning bolt after fireball rocked every scale on his body.

Nath punched. Clawed.

The dark dragons bit and spat.

"Get off me!"

He grabbed hold of a bull dragon and busted its wings. He ripped a grey scaler off his leg and smashed it into the stony ground.

The valley had become a furious knot of muscle and scale gone mad.

A sky raider almost as big as him landed on him and spat hot lava in his face.

Nath rammed it with his horns and blasted it with fire of his own.

It screamed and then withered away.

Shaking his back, he slung a small horde off him.

This is madness! Guzan's beard! They're everywhere!

Bigger, stronger, faster than all of them, Nath tried to take them out one at a time. Tooth and claw penetrated his scales. Dragon blood dripped everywhere. For every two he downed, four more appeared from the frenzied dragon horde.

"Enough of this!"

He gathered his feet under him, spread his wings, and took to the air. He made it up one hundred feet, then two.

Zazz-zap! Zazz-zap! Zazz-zap! Zazz-zap!

The blue razor's lightning ripped through him. Smoke and explosions filled the air. One by one, two by two, and four by four, dragons latched on, pinning his wings, tearing at his body and his legs.

"No!"

Nath twisted out of control and plummeted toward the rushing ground below. He hit one of the arches in the great stone square and plowed right through it. Through the smoke and haze, pushing the rubble and crushed dragons aside, he rose to his feet once more, great shoulders slouched. Aching. Exhausted.

A bright red bull dragon swooped right at him and unleashed its fiery breath.

Nath unleashed his.

The forces collided and exploded.

Boom!

The bull dragon made a rough landing and shook its head. Nath's breath scorched it into the earth, leaving only bones among the ashes.

Nath staggered back and braced himself against the towering stones, feeling empty inside from head to toe. His fire was gone, and he had little breath at all remaining. He glanced up at the sound of the roaring dragons that now descended by the dozens like a swarm of angry hornets.

He lifted his fists and lowered his chin, prepared for his final stand.

CHAPTER

22

"WE HAVE TO GET DOWN there and help him!" Brenwar said, eyeing the sky.

Dragons were pouring down into the valley like rain, and their breath weapons were lighting up the air.

Brenwar's chest tightened. It seemed like the entire world was assaulting his friend, Nath Dragon. "Do something, wizard!" he commanded. "Teleport us or something!"

"Patience," Sasha urged. "He's trying."

Bayzog's eyes were locked on a scroll. His lips moved quickly and spoke at a hastened pace, the words ancient and in Elven.

"Now is not the time for talk! It's the time for action."

"I'm with you, Brenwar," Ben said, rolling his shoulder and checking his arm. He tossed the potion vial to Rerry. "It'll mend you and make you feel great. Finish it." He unhitched Akron from his back. *Clatch. Snap. Clatch.* He tested the string. "Let's go, Brenwar!"

"Don't be foolish," Shum said, stepping in front of them. "Patience. There's nothing but dragons and death down there."

"Get out of our way," Brenwar growled. "Dragons. Death. Aye. And our friend is in it. Move!" He had started to shove past when Hoven stepped in as well.

"Patience!" the Roamer urged. "See what Bayzog unfolds."

"Not when I'm this close," Brenwar said, pushing his way through.

Ben fell into step behind him. "Dead or alive, I'll see you where the battle is."

Suddenly, Bayzog's violet eyes filled with light and radiated with power. His Elven words cut short. The wind picked up like a storm. A black vortex-like tunnel opened up a dozen yards behind him.

"This will take us there," Bayzog said. "Exactly where we'll come out, I'm not certain." He picked up the Elderwood Staff and grabbed Sasha's hand. "Stay here, love."

"I can't," she said, shaking her head. "I'm in this with you to the end."

"We all are," Rerry and Samaz said together.

Bayzog took a deep breath and nodded. "Brenwar!" he yelled out, "lead the way, then!"

Black beard streaming over his shoulder, Brenwar was the first one through the hole. No one was close behind him.

"I've never seen him move so fast before," Ben said, rushing after him. "But we'd better catch up—"

A large bronze dragon dropped out of the sky and blocked the path into the vortex.

"Move," Bayzog yelled, raising his staff and summoning its power.

Hot fire blasted from the dragon's mouth, bouncing off Bayzog's shield and scattering everyone.

The nearby trees erupted into flames.

Shum and Hoven burst into action. One Dragon Needle caught the bronze dragon in the neck.

Its tail whipped out and sent Hoven flying.

Ben fired two arrows.

Twang-Thunk! Twang-Thunk!

The moorite arrows sank into its chest, just missing its heart.

The dragon filled up another lungful of air.

Sprinting out of nowhere, Shum rushed in and lanced his Dragon Needle through its heart.

Its glowing eyes flashed, and its great hulking form toppled over into the vortex—which was no longer there.

"Oh no!" Ben said. "It's gone!"

All eyes gazed from the overlook down to where the battle in the crescent-moon valley raged.

"What do we do?" Sasha said to Bayzog.

He shook his head with disbelief. "I have no idea."

Fallen Foes: Kryzak

CHAPTER
23

NATH SWATTED HIS TAIL. HE punched. Kicked. Grabbed two grey scalers by their necks and slammed their horns together. They wilted in his grip, and he tossed them aside and prepared for the next onslaught.

Fire and lightning raced down from above, pelting him. It seared his smoking scales. Two sky raiders dropped out of the sky and flanked him. Tails coiled around his legs, they tried to pull him down. Another bull dragon landed, charged, and rammed him.

Nath toppled over, shaking the ground.

Thoom!

Small dragons swarmed him like a hive of angry bees. They pinned themselves to his arms and legs. They bit and clawed. Razor-sharp talons tore at his scales. Acid, fire, and jolts of lightning spewed from their mouths.

Nath swatted at them and peeled them off, but his strength was fading.

Keep fighting! Keep fighting!

He gave it everything he had, but their numbers and strength were overwhelming. Claws dug into his ribs. Teeth bit into his legs. It was excruciating. He let out a painful gasp as a dragon stuck a pointy tail into his neck.

Somewhere, he swore he heard Gorn Grattack laughing.

His vision began to fade.

Keep fight ...

His body gave.

Krang!

A bull dragon wailed an awful awakening sound.

Krang! Krang!

A clamor of hisses erupted from the dragons.

Krang! Krang!

Nath opened his battered eyes and spied a small bearded hurricane unleashing his full fury.

"Brenwar?"

"Get off yer scaly behind, Nath Dragon!" Brenwar roared. He brought his war hammer full circle and crushed a snapping dragon's face. *Krang!* "I can't do this alone!" *Krang! Krang! Krang!* He pounded three grey scalers into submission and whirled to face the wrath of the busted-horned sky raider. "Haven't had enough, I see!" Brenwar hefted the war hammer over his head and slung it into the dragon's chest full force.

The missile of moorite howled through the air.

Ka-Chow!

The dragon roared and tumbled.

Nath was on his feet, heart pumping and legs churning, fighting through the frenzy to help his friend. "Look out, Brenwar!"

"What?" Brenwar said, turning around as he retrieved his hammer.

Another sky raider stood behind the battle with jaws the size of a tunnel stretched open.

"Don't you dare!" Brenwar said, shaking his fist at it.

The great dragon's mouth came down, and Brenwar disappeared inside.

Gulp!

"Brenwar! Nooooo!" Nath fell to his knees.

The dragons pounced.

Angry and disheveled, his thoughts a blur, he fought on until his last ounce of great strength was gone and the dragons once again pinned his trembling, broken body down.

I gave it all. I swear I did.

He felt his body being dragged over the ground as he stared weakly into the sky. He saw dragons, black winged and tailed, circling everywhere. Their eyes were green and glowing as they swooped in and out of the clouds around the Floating City.

I should have killed Gorn when I had the chance. I failed.

A flash of gold streaked through the sky. A blurred streak of silver followed. A clamor of roaring dragons filled the air like roaring thunder.

What is happening?

A tight-knit wedge of golden flare dragons sliced through the dark-winged ranks. Two gold dragons peeled off the rear of the wedge and tore a sky raider's wings asunder.

Can it be? Can it be?

A score of silver shade dragons breathed lightning bolts that blasted blue razors out of the air. The swift strike caught the evil dragons off guard, and the wave cut through them like ribbons. Seconds after the chaos, the evil dragons rallied. Gathering their superior forces, they chased the gold and silver dragons through the sky.

The golden flares and silver shades disappeared into the clouds.

Nath felt his excited heart begin to sink.

And I thought they were going to rescue me. I should have known better. I rescued them and they never even thanked me. Why would they save me now?

Out of the clouds another dragon appeared, bigger than a sky raider, pewter with purple scales and dark-red wings. His rack of horns looked like a helmet on his battle-scarred head. Magnificent was an understatement for the grand beast.

Nath sat up gaping.

The dragons that held him released him and leapt into the sky.

Is that? It cannot be!

It was. An immense flying dragon almost bigger than the land-dwelling hulls. A strange flap of scales on his chin made him look bearded. Underneath his scales were knots of rippling muscles like the bull dragon's. He blasted out a roar that drove the dark dragons away, and his grand rack of horns flared like firelight.

Rising to his feet, Nath felt his heart speed up again. *It is him.* "Great Guzan! You live!"

Guzan was the greatest dragon fighter of all. Most believed him to be a man or a dwarf, but he was all dragon, armed with tons of fury and devastation.

The dark dragons were feeling his wrath now. A rush of flame engulfed an entire flock of grey scalers and dropped them from the air.

"Yes!"

Guzan wasn't alone, either. The golden flares zipped out of the clouds, not a dozen but a hundred this time. The silver shades erupted from the mist in the same manner. There was an accompaniment of rose blossoms, green lilies, yellow streaks, blazed ruffies, steel dragons, and many others of all shapes and sizes.

Guzan led the charge, and the sky erupted in scintillating colors of flame.

Nath blinked and shook his head.

They came!

Only one dragon could have command so many.

With an exhausted sigh, Nath dropped to a knee. "Thank you, Father. Thank you, Balzurth."

He spread out his wings and started to flap. "Ow!"

His wing bones were busted, and the skin between them was torn.

"I need to help. I need to fight."

He tilted his head up and watched the carnage in the air. Dragons were dropping from the sky and crashing into the earth. Good dragons, bad dragons, they plummeted, spiraled, and spun out of control. Never in Nath's worst dreams could he have imagined such a horrible scene. The good dragons were taking it to them, in the air and on the ground. Trees shattered into splinters and hilltops burned.

It was war.

It went on for minutes that seemed like an hour.

Suddenly, the dark dragons retreated. They darted for the Floating City and disappeared within the buildings. The Floating City quickly began drifting away under a power of its own. The good dragons did not give chase.

"Finish them!" Nath yelled. "Finish them!"

He locked eyes with Guzan. The ancient dragon's scales were torn, and his wings beat with effort.

Guzan nodded, turned, and led the surviving dragons away.

Nath could hear Guzan's voice inside his head.

This battle is won, but the war is not over. Prepare yourself, Nath Dragon.

Nath surveyed the smoking carnage. Just like men after a battle, dragons lay dead everywhere. Broken. Busted. Bleeding. Scores of them had died. Perhaps hundreds. His head ached and his body shuddered. When he gazed into the sky once more, the good dragons were gone and the Floating City was disappearing over the next mountaintop. He could feel that Gorn was inside the Floating City. Plotting. Hiding.

"This isn't over."

He pushed away the carnage until he located Selene's broken form lying near the throne. She seemed so small and fragile. He shrank down to his man-sized body. Only mildly surprised to find his clothes magically on him again, he kneeled down and brushed Selene's hair aside. His chin touched his chest, and tears filled his golden eyes.

CHAPTER

24

S HUM AND HOVEN LED THE party down the
mountain, through the spreading smoke and
flames, toward the towering rocks. Everyone
was quiet, and Sasha held Bayzog's hand tightly.
He had no idea what to expect when he arrived
down there, but he sensed the danger was gone for
now. But what about Nath and Brenwar?

Witnessing a full-scale dragon battle for the
first time had left his senses jangled. He felt so
small and insignificant. At the same time, he
couldn't make out whether the good dragons had
won or lost. The battle had ended abruptly, with
both parties moving on.

The Roamers stopped and signaled for everyone
to stay back. Hoven pulled back some branches.
Shum stepped though. A copper dragon with black
wings lay on the ground wounded. Its wings and

legs were broken. Using his spear, the Dragon Needle, Shum put it out of its misery, and the party moved on.

Branches crackled and pine cones popped, the flames were so hot.

"This entire mountain will be ablaze soon enough, Bayzog," Ben said. "It's spreading."

"Have you ever seen an entire mountain burn?" Bayzog said.

"Well, no," *cough-cough*, "I haven't."

"Have faith, then," Bayzog said, "and we should be safe in the green grasses of the valley. Make haste now."

When they were nearing the bottom and making their way onto the main path, a strange humming pricked Bayzog's ears. Shum and Hoven turned and looked back at him and nodded. All around where the flames licked at the trees, strange insect-like creatures snuffed them out.

"Do you see that?" Rerry said with wide eyes. "They're putting the flames out."

"It's fairies and pixlyns doing that," Samaz added.

"You don't know," Rerry said, limping along and bracing himself with the Elderwood Staff. His hand snatched out and caught some sort of fly. He opened his palm.

A tiny winged woman sat inside with her arms crossed over her chest, frowning.

"Er ... sorry," Rerry said with a smile.

She stuck her tongue out and buzzed away.

"Told you," Samaz said. "Pixlyns."

Rerry didn't argue.

They made it through the flames into the valley and traversed between the massive stones, searching for any signs of Brenwar and Nath.

Passing through the largest portal, Bayzog noted the massive stone throne, big enough for a titan. Nath Dragon stood beneath it, cradling a black-scaled woman in his arms. His head was down, and tears were streaming down his face. His powerful chest and shoulders shivered, and a brisk wind blew his tangled red mane over his face.

"I've never seen such a look about him before," Sasha whispered to him. Sasha slipped her hand out of Bayzog's and quickly made her way toward Nath. "Nath," she said. "Are you all right?"

Nath didn't respond.

Sasha glanced back at Bayzog and shrugged.

Gorlee found his way to Bayzog's side and whispered in his ear, "That's the High Priestess, Selene."

"She's dead," Nath said, abruptly. "And it's my fault. She saved me. I should have saved her."

"Easy, Nath," Sasha said. She reached over and rubbed his shoulder. "You're alive, and I cannot hide the joy I feel from that." She smiled. "It will be fine. Don't be so hard on yourself. I'm sure you did all you could."

Nath's face, marred with strain, frowned. His chin trembled when he said, "Brenwar's gone."

Bayzog felt his heart sink. Pilpin gasped. Even the Roamers' chins dipped down.

"It's my fault," Nath said. "All my fault. I battled Gorn. I had him. I lost." His head shook sadly from side to side. "I learned a hard lesson today: never let up on evil."

A moment of silence followed.

Bayzog contemplated things. The strained expression on Nath's face told him a horrible story. His friend was wrought with guilt and failure. But the fight wasn't over yet. He needed to lift Nath up. They could regroup. Fight again soon enough.

Pilpin waddled up to Nath. "Can you tell us what happened to Brenwar?"

Nath set Selene down and wiped his eyes. He swallowed a lump in his throat and said, "I was near my end when he arrived and saved me. He took out several dragons, and then a sky raider swallowed him. When the gold dragons arrived, that sky raider took to the sky." He surveyed the carnage. "Now the sky raider is either dead or inside that city with my friend in his belly." He kneeled down and rested his hand on Pilpin's shoulder. "I'm so sorry."

"Humph," Pilpin said. "I'm not worried about

his death. He'd die for you, for me, for dwarven kind at least a hundred times. It's his funeral I'm concerned about. We can't have one without a body. I have to find that dragon. His body." He rubbed his bearded chin. "Sky raider, you say. I seem to remember quite a few of them falling." Pilpin sauntered off.

Hoven followed.

Nath sat down and buried his face in his hands, weeping.

"And I have to bury *her*."

CHAPTER
25

"WE'LL FIND THE RIGHT SPOT for her," Sasha said, wiping tears from his eyes. "A beautiful one."

"Perhaps he needs some time to mourn," Bayzog said, extending his hand to Sasha.

Nath's thoughts were racing.

"No," Nath said. "I'll feel better looking for Brenwar." He started up and eased back down. "Oof, I'm stiff." He glanced at the torn scales on his arms and legs. "But I'm alive. Just paying for it." Grimacing, he took Bayzog's hand and pulled himself up. "Would some of you mind watching over her while I look?"

"Not at all," Bayzog said. "I'll stay here with my family while the rest of you go and look for Brenwar."

Ben came forward. "I believe this is yours." He held out Fang. "And it's good to see you, Dragon."

"You too, Ben," Nath said, extending his hand. They shook and then he took Fang. The polished dragon pommel was warm in his hand. Invigorating. He caressed Fang briefly and strapped his scabbard around his waist. "I missed the both of you." He noticed two men with strong elven features he hadn't met before. "And this must be Samaz and Rerry?"

"Indeed," Bayzog said. "And that man is…"

"Gorlee," Nath said. "Yes, I know. Glad to see you survived, my friend."

"I'm glad you made it through. I had my doubts when you departed for the valley."

Nath nodded to Shum and Hoven, and they made slight bows in return.

"Well, let's go find Brenwar. As much as it hurts, it will only be worse if we don't give him a proper burial." He glanced at Bayzog. "The next step in this war will have to wait, for now."

"Agreed."

Nath and his friends started off after Pilpin. He'd made it beyond the great stone portal he'd passed through before when his scales began to prickle.

"Nath!" Sasha yelled after him. "Nath!"

He whirled around. Shum and Hoven had their

elven blades ready and had formed a wall in front of Selene. Bayzog and his family had backed off.

"What are you doing?" Nath said, jogging back toward the throne.

Shum and Hoven's expressionless faces didn't speak. Behind them, a monstrous winged ape appeared with Selene in his hulking arms.

"Put her down!" Nath yelled. He started to run, but he was so weak. His legs were like lead, and he was tired. So very tired. "Shum! Hoven! What are you doing?"

Sansla Libor's eyes locked on his. A snarl bared his white fangs. He spread his wings and leapt into the sky.

"No!" Nath said, stretching out his hand, trying to change. "Bayzog! Use your staff! Stop him!"

Bayzog raised the Elderwood Staff over his head but then slowly let it down.

Sansla disappeared into the coming night.

Gathering what strength he had left, Nath rushed over and confronted Shum and Hoven.

"Traitors! What did you do that for?"

"He is our king," Shum said, sheathing his sword. "He knows what is best."

Gold eyes blazing, Nath grabbed Shum by the collar and picked the Roamer up off of his feet. "He's a monster!"

"He is our king!

Nath slung Shum away. "No!" He fell to his

knees and started pounding the ground with his fists. "No! No! No! No! No!" Chest heaving, he said. "Where is he taking her?"

"Where it is best."

"That is not an answer."

"I don't know, but it will be for the best."

"Is he going to bring her back?" Nath said, hopeful now that he remembered, "like he did you?"

"I'm afraid not. His magic only works on Roamers, and at that only every century or so. I was fortunate." Shum rested his locked fingers on his belly. "I'm certain the High Priestess is gone. But evil still lives within her. It must be destroyed."

Head down, kneeling, fists resting on the ground, Nath shuddered a breath. Selene had tormented him. Lied to him. Abused him. Was it even possible for her to be redeemed? Had she really given her life to see Gorn destroyed?

He pushed himself off the ground, swayed, and then straightened himself. All eyes were on him. He could feel the essence of his friends. They were resolute. Determined. Ready. Capable. Patient. Faithful. He lifted his chin and nodded.

"No looking back now," he said. "Let's find Brenwar. I can already hear him complaining about missing his funeral."

CHAPTER 26

T HE MOUNTAINSIDE HAD BECOME A cemetery for dragons. Nath had never seen so many dead before. His stomach turned. It would be a poacher's field day.

"They all need to be buried," he said, picking up a blazed ruffie little bigger than a dog. Its orange scales still had a bright sheen to them.

"Won't the dragons return and take care of that?"

Nath shrugged and laid the dragon corpse back down. It made little sense to see dragon fighting dragon. No more sense than seeing men fighting men. Sure, dragons didn't always get along with one another, but they weren't prone to killing each other, either. *No wonder the last dragon war was so horrible.* And by the looks of things, this one would be worse. He had to end it.

"Come! Come!" Pilpin said somewhere deep in the forest.

Nath limped through the trees toward the sound of the dwarf's voice and found a sky raider in a patch of broken trees. His body still smoked, and his scales were in cinders. Both his horns were broken.

"Guzan must have taken this one," Nath said, cocking his head and looking at its eyes.

"Does it look like the one that ate Brenwar?"

Nath shrugged his shoulders. "I don't know."

"I've never seen such a huge dragon before," Rerry said. He put his hands on the dragon's head, which was bigger than a horse. "They seem smaller in the sky and so much bigger up close." He swallowed and looked at Nath. "I'm sorry about your friend." Using the pommel of his sword, he tapped on one of the dragon's teeth, which were almost as tall as him. "One swallow, huh?"

"Rerry!" Sasha admonished. She took her son by the arm and led him away.

"Is it dead?" Ben said, cocking his head. "I swear I think it's still moving."

"Sometimes a dragon's body, being so big, doesn't go right away. It fights, but it will pass."

"I can hear inside it," Pilpin said. He had his ear pressed against the dragon's great belly. "It sounds hungry, the way it's groaning. Let's cut it open. I say Brenwar is inside there, giving it a sour stomach."

Again, all eyes fell on Nath, and he wasn't certain what to say. With some effort, he shrugged again. "Do what you have to do."

Shum and Hoven walked over and unleashed their elven blades. Nath turned away. He abhorred the thought of any dragon being carved into, but he hated the idea of his friend being in there more.

"What's that?" Rerry said.

Nath turned. With a sparkle in his eye, the young part elf was staring at the dragon's great neck. The scales were rippling.

"A spasm," Nath said. "I'm certain."

The spasm started at the lower end of the dragon's neck near the belly and moved upward.

"Strangest death spasm I ever saw," Shum said, tilting his head.

A knot of rippling scales made its way toward the head.

"It's still alive," Rerry said.

"I bet its fire's coming back up," Nath added, following the moving bulge. "Everyone should stand clear. His body might buck, and the entire forest might go ablaze." The moving stopped in the next instant, and with bated breath everyone was silent.

Nath stepped in front of the mouth.

"Be careful, Nath," Sasha said, gripping Bayzog's arm.

"I hear something," Nath said, looking at Shum. "Can you hear it?"

Shum rested his ear on the dragon's upper neck. "It sounds like horrendous singing."

"Singing?" Ben said. "What song is it singing?"

"I'm not sure," Nath said, leaning closer, "wait …. It can't be."

Inside the dragon echoed a song that gave his white scales chills.

Home of the dwarves—Morgdon. Home of the dwarves—Morgdon!

We have the finest steel and ale—Morgdon! In battle we never fail—Morgdon!

Nath's jaw dropped.

Kapow!

The dragon's teeth shattered, leaving a gaping hole between them. Coated in dragon saliva, Brenwar stepped through the gap and slugged the dead dragon in the nose with his hammer.

"Nothing swallows a dwarf and lives!"

"Brenwar!" Nath cried.

Brenwar wiped the slime from his eyes and shook his bearded face like a dog. "Aye!"

"Brenwar!" Pilpin exclaimed.

"Brenwar!" injected Ben, rushing toward him.

Nath scooped his slime-coated friend up in his arms and hugged.

Brenwar eyed him. "Put me down, Nath Dragon."

Nath squeezed him harder. "I know, I know. 'Never hug a dwarf.'"

More than a mile away from the battle site, the party came to a stop and set up a small camp. The smell of death and battle didn't reach this far. The smoke from the burning trees had faded. The pixlyns and fairies had done their job and disappeared back into the woodland.

Ben, Samaz, and Rerry returned with cut branches in their arms. They dropped them by the circle of stones Brenwar had set. The dwarven warrior patted the pouches outside his armor and growled.

"Sultans of Sulfur! That foul beast swallowed my striking stones." He got up. "I'll fetch them."

"Brenwar, please," Nath said. "Sit. I think I can handle it."

Brenwar lifted a brow. "Is that so?"

Nath rubbed his index finger and thumb together, igniting a ball of orange flame. "Toss those sticks in there," he said.

Brenwar did.

Nath flicked the ball of flame, igniting the wood. In seconds, it began to crackle and pop.

"That feels good," Sasha said, nearing the fire and rubbing her shoulder. "I haven't felt warmth for days." She glanced at Bayzog. "Excluding your company of course."

Bayzog showed a quick smile and turned to Nath. "You should save your powers. You need rest."

"I'm tired, no doubt," Nath said, stretching out his arms and yawning.

Bayzog's violet eyes widened.

"What?" Nath said. "It's been a long day."

"We need to discuss things," Bayzog said. "Many things."

"Let's break some bread first," Nath said. "I'm sure everyone is hungry."

Bayzog bowed a little. "As you wish."

Nath combed his fingers through his mane and let out a sigh. Everyone needed rest. Clearly everyone had been through some dire things. Still, Nath felt better than he had earlier. Watching his bristling friend Brenwar grumble orders at everyone did his heart good. Losing Selene was one thing, but losing Brenwar might have been unbearable. He couldn't be happier that his friend was alive.

Edging away from camp, he let the others go about their business. Bayzog and Sasha produced food and water. Ben, Rerry, Samaz, and Pilpin stuffed their faces. Shum and Hoven were nowhere to be found, but Nath could sense them nearby, watching in the woods for other dangers. And Brenwar, he leaned against a rotting stump and stuffed tobacco into a small pipe.

You can judge a dragon by the friends he keeps.

Bayzog had told him that. Nath painted a mental image of the scene and locked it away in his mind. Quietly they ate, speaking little, and before long they bedded down for rest. Sasha was the first asleep, covered in a dark-green blanket with her pretty face turned toward the fire. Rerry and Samaz lay on either side, and Bayzog sat behind them, staring into the fire.

Ben was lying down and talking to Pilpin. Seconds later, he fell asleep mid-syllable. Pilpin snorted, "How rude," and waddled away. He stopped and started talking to Gorlee, who hadn't said much of anything to anyone at all.

The forest became alive with nature song. Soothing. Strong. They were safe for now. Above, the moonlight cut through the dark leaves, darkening the shades around the camp. Through the foliage, Nath saw dragons streak through the night in winks of gold and silver. Balzurth's forces were with them after all.

Still stiff limbed, Nath slipped into the forest. He passed through a clearing and stopped at another rocky overlook. His keen eyes searched the lowlands, looking for any bad signs at all.

Booted feet crunched up behind him. "Not thinking about running off again, are you?"

"Certainly not," he said, turning around and facing Brenwar.

"I think you said that last time."

"No, not with such certain effect."

"Adverse effect is more like it," Brenwar said, puffing on his pipe. "The Truce. Pah!"

"Well, it's over now. You should be relieved."

"I am," Brenwar said. "But I'm more relieved to have you back in my line of sight. And I aim to keep it that way until the end. Do you understand me, Nath Dragon?"

"I do ... now." Nath yawned.

"Stop doing that," Brenwar said as he blew three rings of smoke.

"Why?"

"I don't like it. It makes me jittery."

"*You?* Jittery?"

Brenwar grunted. "Just don't go running off again, Nath Dragon. We have a war to win, and we need you to win it. I think you need us, too." Brenwar turned to walk away. "I'm certain of it."

"I'm not going anywhere," Nath said. "I promise."

Brenwar stopped and turned. "That's a first. You've never promised me before. I think you've finally learned the importance of keeping your word."

Nath smiled, covered his yawn with his elbow, closed his tired eyes, and fell down. He didn't hear what Brenwar said next.

"Sultans of Sulfur! Not again. Bayzog! He sleeps again!"

CHAPTER

27

DREAMS. NIGHTMARES. LIGHT. DARKNESS.
Nath's slumber was nothing short of
restless. He saw Nalzambor burning and
revived. Armies decimated: men, elves, dwarves,
orcs, gnolls, lizard men, goblins, all races. Cities
and towns were torched and burned. Giants
marched over the wasteland. The dark dragons
soared toward Dragon Home. The last of the good
dragons were gathered there. So he dreamed.

Nath's eyes popped open. Hay tickled his nose.
He struggled against his unseen bindings.

What is this?

The last thing he remembered was talking to
Brenwar.

What's going on? How long did I sleep this time?

He squirmed, but the chains around him did
not give.

Moorite!

Scenario after scenario rushed through his thoughts. Was he captured? Imprisoned? Where were his friends? How much time had passed? Another twenty-five years? A hundred maybe?

Guzan, no!

He fought harder against his bonds until he gathered his wits about him.

Why am I covered in hay?

He concentrated. Eased his breath. Listened. He heard the wheels of a cart rolling beneath him.

Am I in a cart?

He sniffed the dampness in the air. Heard heavy footsteps. The distant chirping of birds.

At least I'm outside, not inside. That's a good thing, I think.

He listened longer to the wheels rumbling over a rough road that made them bounce and jangle other things.

Who in Nalzambor is pulling this thing? And why am I in a hay cart?

The golden fibers tickled. He twitched his lips. Crinkled his nose.

Don't sneeze. Don't sneeze.

Nath didn't have any idea if he was among friends or enemies. He pictured draykis in his mind. Perhaps lizard men.

"Achoo!"

The cart came to an abrupt stop.

Great Guzan!

Footsteps approached.

Nath's body went taut. He flexed his muscles against the tight chains. He had to burst free. He felt hands feeling their way around in the hay. Clump after clump was being pulled off him. A rough hand dusted off his face. Nath held his eyes shut. Held his breath.

Let them think they were hearing things.

He could feel light on his face. Sunlight. The figure that loomed over him blocked out a portion of the light. A stiff finger poked his cheek. Poked his nose. A staff of some sort, or maybe a sword hilt, poked at his ribs. Nath didn't flinch. The person continued the poking and prodding.

Enough already!

He heard a sigh that sounded like a man's. A moment later, the figure covered him up again.

That was close. I think.

Nath wanted to wait things out before he revealed himself. He needed to know more about his captor.

But why did he sigh?

The cart lurched forward. The rumbling of the road began anew. Nath's nose began to tickle again, too.

Uh oh, I can't hold it, again!

"Achoo!"

The cart stopped and hasty feet rushed over.

145

Handfuls of hay were scraped from his body. Fingers poked at his face.

Oh, enough of this game!

Nath popped his eyes open and said, "Boo!"

"Dragon!" a friendly voice exclaimed.

"Ben?" Nath said, squinting. Ben's face was hidden behind a beard mixed of brown and grey. The thick muscles of his shoulders were leaner, the armor on his body looser than it had been before. Still, Ben's happy countenance was in there. Nath dreaded his next answer. "How long has it been?"

"Seventy—"

"Seventy years!"

"No, no," Ben said, waving his comment off. "So sorry. Seven years, Dragon. Seven. Sorry, but it's been so long since I've spoken. My tongue was confused by the question."

Nath felt the slightest bit of relief, but still … "Seven years?" He swallowed. "Ben, get me out of here! And why am I chained up like a prisoner?"

"Bayzog's idea," Ben said, raking off the hay.

"That figures. And where is Bayzog?"

"I don't know."

"What do you mean, you don't know? When was the last time you saw him?"

"Uh, almost seven years ago."

"Ben, just get me out of these chains, will you!"

"Hold on now, I have to find the key. Or remember the word."

146

Ben shuffled around the cart, looking for something, and Nath lost sight of him. He could see the cloud-darkened sky, but that was about all.

"Ben, will you at least sit me up so I can take a look around?" Nath huffed. "Seven years? Where is everybody?"

Ben climbed into the cart and propped him up. He hugged Nath. "I can't believe you're back! It feels like it's been a hundred years."

"Ben, what's going on?" Nath scanned the area. The landscape didn't seem familiar. A faint road followed alongside the hills and mountains. Few leaves were left on the branches, yet the weather was warm. The tall grasses, normally the color of golden wheat, were grey. "And where are we?"

"North of Quintuklen," he said, wrestling with the lock on Nath's bonds. "Or what's left of it."

"Left of it? What do you mean by that?"

"They destroyed it."

"You mean, Go—"

"Don't say his name!" Ben whispered harshly. "Never utter it!"

"Fine, but what happened to Quintuklen?"

"Not more than a week after you fell asleep, the Floating City drifted to Quintuklen and burned it to the ground." Ben looked him in the eyes. "Maybe one in ten remain in the ruins. All the rest are dead."

"Get me out of these bonds!"

147

"It seems I'm missing the key."

Nath snorted out a blast of fire. "What was Bayzog thinking?"

"He couldn't have you squirming around. Said something about you moving too much could upset the cart's magic."

"Magic?"

"Sure, it conceals you and me from prying eyes. I keep moving you, from town to town, farmland to farmland. I get stopped a lot. The lizard men and draykis poke and prod a lot."

"A habit you picked up."

"Huh?"

"Never mind," Nath said. "So you've been pulling me all over Nalzambor?"

"Bayzog says they won't search for you in the open, and it's worked up until this point."

"And you've been doing it all alone?"

"Yep."

Nath was moved. Ben was only a man, and seven years was a long long time in a man's life. Hauling a cart along. Day in and day out. For his protection.

"I'd hug you if I could, Ben. Thanks."

"You're welcome," Ben said. "Ah, here's the key."

"Say, Ben, why didn't the army of Barnabus kill you? I thought they were after humans."

"They don't see me as a man." He shrugged and

held out a small talisman. "It's from the chest. It took some getting used to, but it works. It makes me look like a half orc, I think. Hmmm."

"What now?" Nath said.

"Seems I'm having trouble with this lock. It's rusted, jammed, or something."

Nath gasped.

"What?" Ben said, drawing his sword and checking the skies. "What do you see?"

"My scales. They—They've changed color!"

Indeed they had. No longer black, they were pearly white, woven with gold and flecked with red.

Ben smiled. "Yes, and that was years ago. I thought you'd wake up when they changed, but you didn't."

Nath's dragon heart warmed inside his chest. It told him that somehow, he'd made his wrongs right.

"Oh no," Ben said, pointing. "Get back in the cart, Dragon."

"Why, what's wrong?"

A band of soldiers armored in dark grey metal galloped toward them.

"Riders of Barnabus," Ben said. "And by the looks of them, draykis! Quick, get back under the hay. I can handle this."

"Perhaps you could have, but I think they've already seen me."

CHAPTER

28

"**B**EN," NATH SAID, MANAGING HIS way onto his knees. "We don't need that key." Nath set his jaw and flexed his muscles. The moorite chains started to groan, pop, and stretch.

Eyes widening, Ben gasped, "You're bending the moorite."

Chink. Chink. Snap!

The loose chain fell into the hay around Nath's feet.

"Cover yourself up, Dragon," Ben said. "They're looking for you."

In the distance, Nath could see the riders coming hard. Indeed, the five of them were draykis, and the sight of them churned his blood now more than ever before. He inspected the garb he was covered in. A hood covered most of his head, but the cloak that covered his scales hung open. Grabbing a length of moorite chain and tying it around his waist, he stepped out of the small cart and stood by Ben.

"That's a lot of draykis," Ben said, slowly shaking his head. "I've never encountered more than one before, Dragon. We can't let them know who you are. If one gets away, the entire army of Barnabus will be on us."

Narrowing his eyes, Nath said, "Good." He then reached into the cart and filled his hands with the other length of chain.

"Brenwar's not going to be happy that you busted his chain," Ben said.

"When's the last time you saw him?"

"Five years ago," Ben said, "And it's been pretty peaceful since."

Nath stepped in front of Ben. "When this is over, you have a lot of explaining to do. Now wait here."

Nath started up the road. The closer the draykis came, the harder his heart pounded. He could feel the evil. His aversion was enhanced like never before. In the past, their presence had been bothersome, but now that his scales had turned white, they were downright intolerable. Nath draped the chain over his neck and tucked his scaled hands into his cloak.

The draykis pulled their horses to a stop a mere

twenty feet away. Their faces were covered in a patchwork of scales, and tiny horns cropped up on their heads. They were big and endowed with thick layers of muscle. Tongues licked from the mouths of half-dead, half-dragon men. One by one, they dismounted and gathered around Nath in a circle. All of them were tall, but not as tall as him. They wielded heavy, crude swords, clubs, and axes.

Nath jangled his chains. "I've some moorite to sell. Are any of you lizard faces interested?'

"You jest, mortal?"

"I'm only breaking the tension in the air. I'm not sure what to call your kind, but I've heard many things: smelly serpents, clawed ogres, ugly fiends, dragon rumpkins... Hah! The children use that one. Yes, it's all in jest, of course."

"We are draykis. We are death," the leader said. It had a jagged scar on its bare chest. Its spiked metal shoulders were heaving. "Hand over those chains."

"You'll have to pay first, and I don't think we've discussed a price."

One of the draykis shoved Nath from behind.

"Last warning, mortal."

"I don't seem to recall the first warning, so how can that be the last?"

Another hard shove from behind knocked Nath to the ground. He lifted his chin, gold eyes blazing. "You shouldn't have done that." He took the chain from his neck and tossed it at the draykis's feet. He undid the chain around his waist and tossed it aside as well.

The draykis laughed. "Not so mouthy now, are you?"

"Look at his hands," another draykis said. "They have claws and scales."

"What?"

Nath rose to his feet, lowered his hood, and dropped his cloak. The wind bristled his mane of red hair.

"Nath Dragon!" the leading draykis said, gaping. It recovered quickly and said to the others, "Kill him!"

Perspective can change in an instant.

One moment, Ben was slinking behind the cart and gathering Akron, ready to defend his friend, the outnumbered dragon. In the next, he was gaping in wonder.

Nath transformed. In seconds, he went from a seven-foot man to a thirty-foot dragon. Great horns and wings sprouted as he turned into the fiercest, most majestic creature Ben had ever seen. Nath's tail whipped out.

Wupash!

It sent two draykis flying, head over scales.

The horses scattered.

The draykis fought back, striking their swords and axes into Nath's scaled armor.

Nath crushed one down into the ground with his paw. Another he crunched in his jaws and slung away. The last one standing turned to run. Nath consumed it with a mouthful of bright-blue flames. One by one, Nath scorched every draykis to the bone. It happened in seconds.

Nath the dragon turned toward Ben and looked down at him. As smoke rolled from his mouth, he said in a great dragon voice, "That felt good."

Trembling the slightest, all Ben could say was, "That was awesome."

"Ah," Nath said, dusting off his hands, "Stomping out evil, one draykis at a time. A good start for my return." He fastened his eyes skyward. "Perhaps it's time we took to some shelter. I sense more danger is near."

"As you say, Dragon," Ben said, unable to contain his smile. He grabbed the handles of the small cart and started to pull. "There's some sanctuary a few miles beyond the next bend. We can hide in there."

Nath nodded as he checked his garments. Once

again, his shirt and trousers were still intact. He eyed Ben. "Something Bayzog did?"

"I believe."

Nath donned his cloak, pulled on the hood, retrieved the chains, and resumed his trek alongside Ben. He felt great. Strong. Mighty.

"That was something else, Dragon."

"Indeed. I can't help but be impressed, myself. I feel so ... free." He glanced at the sky. "You know Ben, I could fly us wherever we need to go."

"I'll pass. I flew on a dragon once already, and my stomach still feels queasy. Perhaps if I was younger." He frowned. "Walking and riding do me just fine."

"When did you ride a dragon?"

"Oh, not long after you slept. She was a very pretty one, too. Gorgeous eyes, pearl-horned with turquoise scales. Something I'll never forget."

"Are you serious? A dragon let you ride her?"

"Rescued us, is more like it. We were trapped. Penned in near Jordak's Pass. We were taking you to a new place to hide. Then wham! Dragons closed in." Ben shook his head. "We escaped, barely. After that, Bayzog came up with another plan."

Nath let Ben continue talking. He studied Ben. His friend's brown hair had become greyish and wispy. There was a hitch in his step and a slight wheeze in his breath. Wrinkles lined his eyes, and more scars marked his face. It seemed like Ben had gone from a vibrant young man to an old iron war horse in an instant. But there was still light in Ben's kind brown eyes and an avid curiosity.

"I see you looking at me, Dragon, but don't fret. I've lived more than I've lost. And I live for what I've lost. My wife. My children. I miss them, but I understand that no matter what, this battle must be fought. And I'm honored I have a part in it, be it a small one or not."

"Ben," Nath said, "you have been everything a friend should be and more. I'm grateful."

"So am I, Dragon. The things I've seen. The adventures we've shared. It's been wonderful. But Dragon?"

"Yes."

Ben looked him right in the eyes. "Promise me we'll finish this before I die."

Always keep your promises, His father always said. *Never make a promise you cannot keep.*

Nath shook his head no. "I wish I could promise you that, but all I can promise is that I'll try my best."

Ben nodded yes. "Well, that's good enough for me."

"Now, Ben, tell me everything I need to know."

CHAPTER

29

BEN WARMED HIS HANDS OVER a small fire just inside the mouth of a cave.

"Every time the sun drops, my bones get cold. And the rain makes my knuckles ache and my scars throb." He glanced at Nath. "Do you have any aches and pains?"

Inside, Nath hurt. Selene had been gone seven years, but it felt like she had died yesterday.

"I'm fine." Nath tossed a stick into the fire. "So get on with it. Where is everyone?"

"Barnabus has the world under its thumb. Men have been wiped out. Women and children enslaved."

"All men?"

"Of course not. But after Quintuklen was stifled, it scattered them all. The Legionnaires that numbered thousands strong are maybe a few hundred now."

It riled him. But men, always so conflicted with one another, were so easily scattered, unlike the other races that clung tightly together.

"Morgdon and Elome work together, though," Ben said, shaking his head in disbelief. "Never imagined they'd team up as they did, but it was either that or annihilation. For seven years they've defended their lands from the wicked humanoid forces. Orcs, gnolls, and goblins swarm over and over. I've seen it for myself.

"Is that where Brenwar and Bayzog are?"

Shrugging, Ben stirred a stick in the fire. "I suppose. But I never know what they're thinking."

"What of the dragons?"

"They still war all over. Some with the races. Others without. It depends. I've seen quite a few while you've been asleep. But the battles are one thing and the search for you is another." Ben combed his fingers through his beard. "Barnabus's forces still search for you. I don't think the dragon warlord is fully committed in his triumph until he knows you're through. Things are at a standstill of sorts. Like the Truce, but worse." His eyes reflected the firelight. "They're sharpening their claws. Holding their foul, furnace-hot breath. Waiting for you to surface."

"I'm here now," Nath said, looking at his hand.

His golden-yellow claws were as sharp as ever. His scales twinkled in the firelight. He was hungry. Hungry for another crack at Gorn Grattack. "So what was the plan once I awakened?"

"Ah," Ben said, nodding. "I almost had forgotten." He yawned. "Or have I forgotten? I haven't thought about that for quite some time." He shook his head. "I'm not so old, am I? Only fifty seasons."

"Ben," Nath said, aggravated, "how did you go about taking turns watching me? Was there a signal? Something? Anything?"

"Normally someone would just show up. Rerry and Samaz did. But now, I'm not so sure. Maybe something happened to them? I can't be certain."

"Ben, do you feel all right?"

"I'm just tired, Dragon. It's been a long day." Ben lay down on his blanket and fell fast asleep.

"Ben?"

Nath was surprised that his friend was out cold. And even more surprised that Ben seemed so old. Something was out of place that he couldn't put his finger on. The world was off. Out of place.

Am I still dreaming?

Ben stirred and rustled in his armor. The beaten breastplate from his brief stint with the Legionnaires had held up quite well. It was good work for something that wasn't dwarven.

Nath grabbed a blanket out of Ben's pack and

covered his friend. He then headed out of the cave to stretch his legs. The air was brisk, and a cool drizzle was coming down. The sensation felt soothing for a change.

Learn to appreciate the little things.

He glanced up the hill. The firelight in the cave was dim. Nath fought the urge to wake Ben back up and ask more questions. He needed to know where everyone was. Where to start? Where to go? It seemed Ben didn't know anything. Perhaps that was by design. It was the best way to keep everyone safe. The less everyone knew, the better. It was the best way to protect Nath and everyone else.

But I can't just stand around. Not after seven years.

Nath wanted to take flight. Get a good look around. He glanced back again.

He never left me. I can't ever leave him. Just let him rest. I'm sure he'll have answers tomorrow. I slept seven years, so what's one more night?

Nath sat on the hillside and reflected on things. He could turn into a dragon now and still just as easily maintain a man's form. He tossed a small ball of orange and blue fire from palm to palm, wondering what other powers he might have. He needed to understand them, but he had no one to teach him. Selene could have, and had to some degree, but she had also deceived him. And where had Sansla Libor taken her? He closed his eyes and took a long draw of breath through his nostrils.

Focus, Nath. Trust your instincts.

He heard Ben's heartbeat, slow, steady, and strong. Animals prowled the night. Pixlyns sang the song of crickets. The gentle wind tickled the leaves. The night could bring terror, but it could also bring peace. He eased his clawed hands into the ground. He felt the trepidation deep in the bowels of the world. Its life was in jeopardy. It was on a course that ended in death.

Where do I resume this battle? Where do I start?

He meditated until the dawn's light caught his face.

He felt an unnatural tremor nearby. A rustle of armor. He cocked his head.

Two men approached on cat's feet. He felt their hearts pounding in their chests.

Thump-thump. Thump-thump. Thump-thump.

Nath remained still.

Let the bandits strike. Their blades can't cut my scales.

The soft shuffles came closer and closer. Nath could feel hard eyes on his back.

"If you're going to kill me," Nath said, raising his arms above his head, "Make it swift."

CHAPTER
30

GORN GRATTACK'S EYES POPPED OPEN. Smoke rolled from his nose. He lifted his ten-foot-tall frame from his throne and stepped down off the dais. Standing as a man, he stroked the horns on his head and spoke to one of the many draykis that guarded the throne room inside the Floating City.

"I sense our enemy has awakened." He lifted his chin toward the glass dome above. "I can feel him." He clenched his clawed fists. "And I hate it."

"Shall I send more out in the search for him?" the winged draykis commander said.

"No, I will see to it that he comes to us. Come."

Gorn's tail slithered behind his back as he headed out of the throne room into the city. Legions of skeleton soldiers waited outside the cathedral that Gorn departed. Their black eyes flared with life and hunger. Gorn's towering frame waded through them and down the street. Above, dragons crowed and snorted. Hundreds could be seen perched on spires and rooftops. Their eyes glowed green with energy. They were under Gorn's control, thanks to the power of the jaxite stones, and for seven years his army had been growing.

He strode down the streets toward the Floating City's edge. A grey-stone building stood in his path, dark and grim. Skeleton soldiers pulled open the tall iron doors as he approached. Unaccompanied, Gorn went in. He stood in the inner courtyard of a small covered prison. There were barred chambers three stories tall, open, most of them abandoned and empty.

Gorn's rough voice echoed in the cold chamber. "I have great news."

Several torches that illuminated the cages that lay in the room flickered at the sound of his voice.

Gorn headed for the largest one in the center. A lone figure leaned against the bars, huddled in tattered robes, shivering. There were other cages, but they were empty. Lying on the stone floor nearby were dragons, grey scalers. Heads down, their tongues slithered from their mouths.

"I said, I have news." Gorn banged on the cage. "Nath Dragon is awake. How does that make you feel? Hopeful?"

From underneath the hood, a pair of violet eyes fastened on Gorn's.

"I'm hopeful? Aren't you, Bayzog?"

The part-elf wizard rose to his feet and coughed. Shackled, he teetered toward the bars, clasped his grubby hands on them, and faced off with Gorn. "The end nears, and I couldn't be gladder."

"I'm thrilled you share my thoughts," Gorn said. "And now it's time to draw out our needle in the haystack."

"I've told you everything. I don't know where he is."

"Don't toy with me, Bayzog! You might not know where he is, but you do know how to find him!"

"We've danced this dance before, to no avail. And it's not my life I'm worried about. Even if I could help, I would never yield."

"No, I'm certain you won't." Gorn snapped his fingers. The iron doors opened, and the draykis marched three hooded figures inside. "But perhaps they will."

Bayzog stiffened.

Gorn stepped back and grabbed the hood on the nearest one. "We recently came across some persons you might be interested in."

Bayzog's eyes shone like moons as he pressed his face against the bars.

Gorn pulled off the hood, and there stood Sasha.

"No!"

"Yes," Gorn replied. He plucked off the other two hoods, revealing Rerry and Samaz. "Tell me how to find Nath Dragon, or I'll make your family pay."

CHAPTER

31

"I OUGHT TO KILL YOU," BRENWAR'S strong voice said, "fer falling asleep again."

Nath twisted around and jumped to his feet. "Brenwar!"

With War Hammer slung across his back, the dwarf stood as tall and stout as ever. His beard was still mostly a prominent black, but more grey had taken over.

Pilpin stood beside him. "Enjoy your nap?"

"It's good to see you, too," Nath said. He stepped forward and clasped Pilpin's hand. "The both of you."

"It's good to see you on your feet, Nath," Pilpin said, combing his beard. "Especially during the exciting times we live in. I'm glad you're back."

Both of the dwarves were worse for wear. Their breastplates were dented, scars raced along their corded arms, and their other garments were tattered and rumpled.

"You knew where to find me, didn't you?" Nath said to Brenwar.

Brenwar pulled a spyglass from his pocket and rattled it in the air. "I wasn't letting you out of my sight no matter what Bayzog said. Not again. I've always been around, and if not me, Pilpin kept an eye out."

"Does Ben know this?"

Brenwar shook his head. "He's a bit daffy after he took a hard shot on the head. A giant clipped him good a while back." Brenwar spied the cave. "Asleep is he? Hmmm."

"He did seem a bit off. Is he all right?"

"He's fine. Just fuzzy on the details of things. Nothing to worry about. He's as good a fighter as ever."

"Are you sure about that?"

"He's fine."

"Perhaps that's why he couldn't tell me anything. I asked and asked, but he was a bit clueless."

Brenwar sank the axe end of his war hammer into a fallen log. "We're here to fill you in. What do you know?"

"It's only been a day ..." Nath proceeded to tell all that Ben had shared. "And I'm eager to get on with things. Where's Bayzog? He still lives, does he not?"

Brenwar looked away at Pilpin, who was staring at him.

"He's dead?" Nath asked.

"No, just missing. It's been a few years."

Nath's heart sank. "What happened?"

"Don't know. We've had a rendezvous set up years in advance and he hasn't been at the last few."

"We think Gor—"

"Don't say it," Brenwar said to Pilpin.

"You really think that?"

"He's not with the elves, and not even Shum and Hoven can find him."

"At least the Roamers are still with us," Nath said. "What about my father? Is he still aiding in all this?"

"Your father's forces thin, Nath, but they still fight. Many have been tempted and taken by that city that floats on the jaxite."

Nath rubbed his forehead and sighed. "Don't you think we should rally one massive army to defeat them?"

"I believe that's where you come in."

"Me?"

"The dragons won't listen to *us*."

"They never listened to me before."

Brenwar eyed his scales. "I've a feeling they will now."

"Perhaps."

"Pilpin, go and rustle Ben up, we need to get moving."

The small dwarven warrior hopped to his feet and scurried away.

"I saw what you did to those draykis," Brenwar said.

"And?"

"You should've had enough sense to bury them. Not long after we came along, others started to pick at them." He scratched his beard. "I don't think it will take long for the forces of Barnabus to figure out you are near."

"You said we needed to get moving. If so, where are we going?"

"You woke up at the right time, it seems."

"Why is that?"

"It's near time for the next rendezvous."

"And where might that be?"

Brenwar rubbed his face and muttered under his beard, "Near the City of Waste and Ruin."

"I've never heard of that."

"Quintuklen."

Nath swallowed. "Ben says the Floating City is there. Why would you pick such a risky place to meet?'

"Because it was still a city when we made the plan. Can't help the fact it's not there now. It's still the plan. Now let's get moving. I've got a strange feeling in my bones."

So do I, Nath thought. *So do I.*

CHAPTER
32

LATE AFTER NIGHTFALL FIVE DAYS later,
traversing harsh elements and avoiding
prowling enemies, Nath and company
arrived a league southwest of Quintuklen. They
had moved day and night, taking little time to
sleep, which only Ben seemed to need. His friend
slept in the cart half the time while Brenwar and
Nath took their turns pulling it.

"I can see it," Nath said, peering skyward.

"See what?" asked Pilpin.

"The Floating City."

It hung like a small moon east of Quintuklen,
mostly hidden by a strange mist. He could see the
jaxite that ebbed with glowing light beneath it.
Dragons darted swiftly through its cloud.

Nath's strange feeling only got stronger. "I can
feel him."

"Him who?" Brenwar said, glancing at the sky.

"Him."

"Aye, I suppose you do."

Nath looked at Brenwar.

Brenwar added, "Being a dragon and all." He set the cart handles down and used his glass to spy the small farm they approached. He readied his axe. "We'll go take a look."

Nath started to object, but Brenwar and Pilpin were too quick to scurry away.

"Great."

He leaned against the cart. Ben lay in the hay, snoring softly. Nath closed his eyes and stretched out his senses. He didn't sense evil or danger. That ability had come in handy as they traveled, alerting them to take cover whenever dark forces approached. It took everything Nath had to hold his powers back. He was eager to unleash them, test them out. It was torture.

What else can I do? I need every edge I can get.

Almost an hour later, he noticed Ben beginning to stir.

"Dragon," Ben said, sitting up in the hay and rubbing his blurry eyes. "Have we arrived?"

"They're checking it out."

Ben slid out of the cart and buckled on his sword. He stretched his arms and yawned. "I wish I didn't get tired, like you."

"Oh, I get tired. I just sleep for years when I

do," Nath said, laughing. "Come on, let's catch up with the others. There's no danger out there waiting."

Together they wheeled the cart toward the farm until they found Pilpin standing outside the barn, waiting.

"I suppose they're inside?"

Pilpin nodded. "Waiting on you. Ben, they want you to stand guard with me."

"I'd rather—"

"I'm sure it's for the best," Nath said, patting Ben's shoulder.

He proceeded inside the barn door, and Pilpin pulled it shut behind him. The ramshackle barn was typical, with stables and a loft. Brenwar sat at a large table lit by a lantern in the middle. Three other figures sat there as well, with hoods pulled over their heads. That strange feeling returned and knotted his stomach. He stopped at the edge of the table.

"Is there a need for secrecy?"

Two of the three cloaked figures that sat across from Brenwar dropped their hoods. It was Shum and Hoven. He almost didn't recognize them. Their faces had been burned by fire and scarred by battle.

"Apologies," Shum said, "we aimed to spare you displeasure."

"Never say such a thing, my friend. I see only

beauty, inside and out. But I hurt from all your suffering on my account."

"It is our honor to serve," Hoven said, adding a smile. "And these marks fill me with honor."

Nath nodded and fixed his eyes on the person at the end of the table. "Are you scarred as well, my friend Bayzog?"

"Nay," Bayzog said, dropping his hood. Tears were in his eyes. He wiped his sleeve on his cheek. "It is my shame that I hide, for I have failed."

"What happened? Where is Sasha? Where are your sons?"

Bayzog rolled a crystal orb down the table. It hopped over the lantern and hovered above.

"It was here when I arrived, two days ago."

It grew and brightened in swirls and colors until a clear image formed. Bayzog's face emerged. He was inside an iron cage. His voice was pleading, "He has us. He has us all."

The image panned backward, revealing the disheveled Sasha, Rerry, and Samaz in small separate cages. Sasha's fingers were stretched through the bars toward her sons and theirs toward hers, but they could not touch.

Nath's heart ignited. "We have to save them!"

The image altered, and Gorn Grattack's terrifying countenance appeared. "I want Nath Dragon's sword, Fang, or all of them die! You have one week." The image vanished.

"Gorlee!" Nath said, pushing his hair back. "That was him, not you!"

Bayzog nodded. "Gorlee went there on his own in hopes of discovering more about the enemy by the time you awoke. That was years ago. This is the first I've seen him." Bayzog sighed. "My family was separated from me, but only recently did I lose track of them. When I saw this, my horrors were confirmed."

"We'll save them, Bayzog." Nath said. "We're here, and we'll go and save them today."

Bayzog shook his head no. "We are not ready to rush into this. Too much is at risk."

"They'll die."

"Perhaps, but they know the risks. We all do. So much is at stake. They'll understand."

"You'll see them alive again," Nath said. "I swear it."

"Nath, heroes and dragons have tried to get in, and none of them have survived. Not one. The Floating City is impenetrable."

Nath rapped his knuckles on the table and stood. "I've been inside it."

Brenwar scowled at Nath.

Bayzog said, "Our kinds are working on something so we can go with you. It's unknown if it's ready yet, but we can check."

"And why did he ask for my sword and not me?"

"I'd say your confrontation is inevitable, but I

don't follow why he would need Fang. It's an odd request," Bayzog said.

A thought struck Nath. "Perhaps it is the only blade that can kill him. I battled him once before, lanced him through the heart. He only laughed."

"He might not have a heart as we understand it," Bayzog said.

"Makes sense," Brenwar added, shrugging his shoulders. "Or maybe he needs it to kill you."

Nath leaned over the table. "Regardless, we have to give it to him."

"Nath, that's too dangerous," Bayzog said.

"Your family is at risk, and time is short. I've made my decision. Where is it?"

The creaking barn doors opened and Pilpin burst through. "I tried to stop them, but eh," he glanced back over his shoulder as two ominous figures entered the barn. The hulking winged figure of Sansla Libor emerged, and beside him stood Selene.

CHAPTER 33

WIELDING HIS WAR HAMMER, BRENWAR rushed between Nath and Selene.

Shum and Hoven stood ready on either side of him.

"The dead rise against us!" Brenwar said. "Stay back, Nath!"

Selene let out a soft chuckle, opened her palms, and took a knee. "I assure you I am not dead, Brenwar Bolderguild. And I'm not here to fight against you, either." She rose back up, eyeing Nath. "I come to join you."

Selene had changed. The hard lines on her face had softened. The black scales that had dressed her body were now lavender mixed with white. Her presence was soothing, almost radiant. And beautiful.

Nath's heart pumped hard inside his chest. He sensed that hers rang as true as there had ever been.

Behind Selene, Sansla Libor let out a grunt.

Shum and Hoven sheathed their swords and backed away.

Nath folded his arms over his chest. "You have much to explain."

"It would be my pleasure." She grabbed the necklace around her neck and pulled it out from underneath her white robes, revealing a brilliant white amulet that illuminated the room.

Everyone shielded their eyes but Selene and Nath.

"The Ocular of Orray!" he said in amazement.

"I died," she said, "but Sansla, Laedorn, and the elves redeemed me."

Nath stepped closer. His eyes slid from hers to the amulet. "Why would they?"

"To help you, I believe." She forced a smile. "The Ocular sustains me so long as it is in my possession. It's temporary."

Nath looked solemnly into her eyes. "You'll die without it?"

"It's uncertain, but most likely." Selene tucked the Ocular back inside her robes. "That's why I need to teach you all that I can in the little time we have left together."

Nath reached out and held her face between his hands. She was warm and more real than she had ever been before. He felt the light within her. "Bayzog, did you know about this?" he said over his shoulder.

"I knew they had her. I did not know she was revived. It's a wondrous thing that the elves would use the Ocular on Selene. A good sign, I believe."

"A great sign." He studied Selene's eyes. "I'm glad you have returned, and I hope it's not temporary."

She squeezed his hand. "So do I."

"Are there any other surprises?"

"Dragon!" Ben said, bursting inside. "Dragon! Come quick!"

Nath rushed outside the barn.

Dragons in flocks like birds were landing in the fields. Their bright eyes and colorful scales twinkled in the moonlight.

"Your army comes," Selene said in his ear. "Are you ready to lead them?"

"Can you feel that?" Selene said to Nath. "What is she thinking?"

It was still nighttime. Nath stood facing a golden flare dragon. She had long lashes over her pretty eyes, and he could feel her heart beating under his fingertips.

"She thinks I'm handsome," he said, showing a broad grin.

Selene rolled her eyes. "Uh-huh, and what else?"

"She's ready to fight. Eager."

"Tell her to do something. Bend her will."

Nath didn't like the sound of that. "I'd rather ask."

Selene folded her arms across her chest. "A general doesn't ask his soldiers to fight in the war. He's a commander. He gives orders."

"True, and they follow a commander they respect even better."

"You're proven, Nath. They wouldn't be here if you weren't."

"Fine." He cleared his throat and spoke in Dragonese. "Golden flare, trip Selene."

The dragon's tail whipped out, making the sound of a cracking whip.

Wupash!

Selene was upended and crashed onto the ground.

Nath nodded in satisfaction. "I think I have it. What other lessons will you teach me now?"

Selene walked him through the steps of changing form. As a man, he grew a tail and wings. He added horns even.

"Fascinating."

She taught him to blow different kinds of

smoke, acid, fire, and even ice. He froze trees and shattered them with ease.

"Summon enough power, and your roar alone can split rock and splinter trees," she said. "But your power is limited. You control great magic and can do many things; just don't overdo it." Her face darkened. "Our enemy is ancient, Nath. He'll tempt you to burn up your powers until you weaken, and then, like a monstrous asp, he'll strike you in the neck, burrow inside your body, and poison the heart within." Her expression became distant. "That's what he did to me."

Nath nodded.

"You surprised him once before," she said. "He won't be caught off guard a second time."

"Could I have killed him then? When I had him?"

"His body maybe, but not his spirit. It takes a special weapon to sever the spirit from the body. That's what Barnabus did."

Nath remembered the legends of the man Barnabus that Bayzog had shown him long ago. Barnabus had wielded a great sword that lanced and banished Gorn after the last Dragon War. Barnabus's heroics had been twisted ever since and turned against the good.

"Do you know what happened to Barnabus and that sword?" Nath asked of Selene.

She chuckled. "Do you not yet know who Barnabus is?"

"No, should I?"

"Yes, you should. Barnabus is your father."

Nath's limbs went numb. "What?" Inside, it all felt true, and then he realized there had been a time when his father was a man, too.

Selene puckered her brows.

So did Nath. "But the sword, Fang, he made for me. Fang can't be the same sword that he used before. Is he?"

"I don't think the last sword did the trick, and I believe your father forged another. I've heard it told that the other blade snapped the last time he used it. It vanquished the dragon warlord, but not entirely."

"So that's why he wants Fang?"

"That blade in the right hands can destroy both body and spirit," she said. "He fears it."

"All this time, I had the key in my claws," he said, eyeing Selene. "And you knew it."

"I suspected."

"Why didn't you try to take Fang, way back when?"

Selene gazed up at the Floating City. "He wanted me to turn your will. With you on his side, the blade's power would have been useless. He took a calculated risk, I failed at my task, and now he just needs the blade." She turned her gaze back to him. "Sorry, Nath."

"I guess I'll have to forgive you," he said, holding her gaze, "but I have one other question. Where is Fang?"

CHAPTER 34

"I'M NOT SO CERTAIN THIS is the best course of action," Bayzog advised. The part-elven wizard held his chin and rubbed his finger under his eye. "The entire world is at stake."

"Where is the sword, Bayzog? I haven't seen Fang since I woke up!" Nath pushed his back off the support post in the barn and unfolded his arms. "This is my choice, not yours. And if I want to save your family at my risk, I will."

Bayzog's violet eyes flashed. "Do not insist that I don't want to save my family, Nath Dragon. I'm considering other options."

"I know you want to save them more than anybody. But we don't have the time. They don't have the time!"

Brenwar stepped between the pair. "All right

now. We're on the same side. But Nath, I'm with Bayzog on this. We can try another way."

Nath stiffened. "I say we give them the sword. Period. Now where in Nalzambor is it?"

Bayzog looked him in the eye and said, "I don't know."

Nath looked down at Brenwar.

"I don't know either."

"Who does know, then?" Nath turned and looked at Ben, who sat on the cart sharpening his sword. "Ben, certainly you know."

Ben scratched his head. "I haven't seen it since ... I don't know, when?"

Nath spun around, looking at everyone. "Well, who was the last one to have it?" He caught Brenwar and Bayzog's eyes meeting and looking away. He raised his voice. "I'll storm the Floating City alone if I must! I'll not fight beside those I cannot trust. And you, Brenwar, always on me about my tales, and now you're telling one yourself. By the Sultans! Sasha, Rerry, and Samaz's lives are on the line!"

"I don't know where it his!" a bristling Brenwar said.

"Nath," Bayzog intervened, "we took precautions so that the sword would never be found unless absolutely needed. I don't know where it is. No one here does."

Nath started to pace. "*What* precautions?"

"When we learned the Dragon Warlord desired

it, we had it hidden." Bayzog fetched his staff from the table and started to walk away. "For exactly this reason."

"So, if I weren't threatening to ransom it to him, would you get it for me?"

"We would, but we can't with your current intent."

Nath's claws dug into his palms. Bayzog was hiding something, but he wasn't lying.

Think like a dragon, Nath. Outwit this wizard.

"I'm sorry, friends," Nath said as Bayzog headed toward the barn doors, "I believe you. You clearly would never lie in such dire times. Whatever you have done, I know you have done it for my protection as well as others. I'm grateful. But ..." Bayzog stopped. "Perhaps I have not been asking the right question. I think I'll ask another. You say you don't know where the sword is, but I now ask, do you know how to find it?"

Bayzog gently nodded and turned. "I do." He glanced at Brenwar. "We need the chest."

Brenwar looked over at Pilpin. Pilpin dug his fingers into one of his pouches and produced a tiny replica of Brenwar's chest. He spoke in Dwarven. "Iidluumkraaduum." He rapped his knuckles on the chest. Its banding crackled and popped, and the chest expanded until it stopped at normal size.

"It's in there?"

"No," Bayzog said, stepping to the chest and

kneeling. He opened the lid and fingered the rows of small vials. He plucked out one filled with liquid the color of plums. "Ben, come and drink this."

"Me?" Ben said, setting down his sword and walking over. "Why me?"

"Because I'm tired of you being daffy," Brenwar said. "Now drink it!"

Ben snatched the vial, popped the cork, and drank it down. He blinked, thumped his chest, burped, and swooned.

Nath reached over and steadied his friend. "What did you give him?"

"I think I need to lie down," Ben said, holding his head. He sagged back in Nath's arms and burped again. He steadied himself. "Maybe not."

"Care to explain, Bayzog?" Nath said.

"We had Ben hide Fang. When he finished, we gave him a potion that makes him forget things. It kept us all innocent in case our enemies captured us. The sword is as safe as it ever was."

"And what if it's in a place so far off we can't get it?" Nath said. "Great Guzan, Bayzog! You overthink these things. Time is pressing. We only have one day."

"Ben," Bayzog said, "where is the sword?"

Ben ambled over to the cart and picked up his sword. "Here it is."

"No, you daffy idiot!" Brenwar said. "Bayzog,

I told you this was a bad idea. He's permanently forgotten."

Bayzog rose up. With a serious tone in his voice, he said, "Ben …. Where is Fang?"

Ben gazed up into the rafters with a glassy look in his eyes.

Brenwar and Pilpin slapped their foreheads. "Oy!"

Nath glared at Bayzog. "Well done, old friend. Well done."

Ben started to laugh.

"What's so funny?" Brenwar said.

Ben slapped his knee and said with a smile on his face, "I know where Fang is." He got down on his hands and knees and crawled underneath the cart.

"He's gone loony," commented Pilpin.

There was a rustle of metal on wood and wood on metal. Something snapped. Ben crawled out from under the wagon and popped up on the other side. He raised his arms high. In one hand he held Fang, and in the other was Akron.

"All this time I thought I lost them, and all this time they've been right under my nose."

"That's the dumbest hiding place ever," Brenwar remarked, tugging at his beard.

Bayzog added with a smile, "Yet brilliant at the same time."

CHAPTER 35

THE FELINE FURY HAD MADE his way to the small farm and gone, only to return hours later. The dragon cat lay on the grass at the feet of Nath, who sat on a stone bench in the garden. It purred, and fragrant petals of smoke wafted from its nose.

"It seems you are making new friends in the dragon world all the time," Selene said, taking her place by his side. "It's comforting to see."

"It certainly is, seeing how you used the fury against me."

Selene bent forward and stroked the great cat's mane. "I raised him. Did you know that?"

Nath shook his head.

"He was my prized hunter. Tracker. One of the most gorgeous dragons I'd ever seen. And even in captivity, these dragons are hard to tame. But I bent him to my will." She glanced up at Nath. "But in the end, it was your will that won him over. Did you know that?"

"No."

"I learned of the fury's deception, Nath. I felt it. It preferred you over me, and for the first time in my life, I doubted myself. I doubted Gorn as well." She locked her fingers inside the fury's mane. "I lost my pet—not out of fear, but out of adoration. I saw for the first time that good things don't take a shine to evil. Your light turned the fury's light on as well. Balzurth is proud."

Nath looked at her. "Have you ever—"

"Met him? No. Never. But I think I have a fine idea what to expect of him."

Down the road, Bayzog and Brenwar approached. The part-elven mage leaned on the Elderwood Staff, and his eyes were still weary. Brenwar frowned over his folded arms.

"They approach," Bayzog said. "Nath, you don't have to go through with this. Not on my account and not theirs. They are willing to die for what is right: saving Nalzambor."

Nath's golden fingertips toyed with Fang's dragon-headed pommel. The mystic metal, no longer hotter than fire, was cool in his hands. The tiny gemstone eyes of the dragons twinkled in the daylight. Fang was one of the most precious things his father had given him, which technically, he should not have. He'd let Brenwar borrow it, and

Brenwar had lent it to him. He stood up, handed the sword to Brenwar, looked at Bayzog, and said, "I have faith."

Brenwar grunted.

Bayzog gave a nod.

Nath came forward.

Brenwar stayed him with his hand. "You wait. We'll deliver this. We meet now in the valley. From up there," he pointed to a crag on a hillside, "you can watch."

Nath started to object but held his tongue. After all, this was his idea. "As you wish, Brenwar." He turned and looked at Selene. "Coming?"

Nath, Selene, and the feline fury made their way to the crag. He couldn't fight off the uneasiness that twisted his belly. Giving up Fang, the only weapon that might kill Gorn Grattack, was a gut-wrenching task, but he had to believe it was the right thing.

"That was a brave thing you did," Selene said. She patted him on the back. "I don't think anyone else in this world would have done that."

Nath's chest tightened. He could see his friends entering the valley, where a score of draykis awaited them, accompanied by half a dozen horse-sized dragons. Behind Brenwar, Pilpin, a hooded Bayzog, and Ben, were Shum, Hoven, and the hulking Sansla Libor. A more than formidable party, but they were vastly outnumbered by a superior force.

"I should be down there," he whispered. "I feel a trap in the works." He started forward.

Selene grabbed his arm. "They'll be fine. Wait it out."

Nath swallowed and eyed her. Selene's dark eyes had a twinkle of excitement in them. Sansla's appearance with Selene had been suspicious. She'd been able to deceive him before. She could certainly do it again. His blood ignited, and he jerked away.

"Nath? What are you doing?"

He peered down in the valley, keen eyes alert to everything. His friends were now surrounded by the draykis and dragons. Brenwar did the talking.

"Don't you move a muscle!"

"All right," she said.

"Not a word, Selene."

The feline fury's purr became a hearty rumble. Nath's senses tingled.

What is going on? Something is going on!

He squatted down on the rock, ready to spring. So much deceit. So much betrayal. He'd somehow talked himself into giving Gorn Grattack everything he wanted. The draykis commander gave a nod. The other draykis led four hooded figures over. They had the builds of Sasha, Samaz, Rerry, and Bayzog.

Shum came forward and removed the hoods.

All their faces were clear: Sasha, Rerry, Samaz, and a part elf that looked like Bayzog.

Brenwar handed over the sword to a winged draykis commander, who eyed the blade.

"Everything is fine." Selene sat down on the rock and added, "You're the one who said you had faith. Now practice it."

Nath clenched his jaw as the dragons crowded the circle. Suddenly, the draykis commander, Fang in hand, took to the sky. Covering the area in a puff of smoke, the dark dragons took flight and escorted the draykis commander back to the Floating City. When the smoke cleared, all the draykis were gone, leaving Nath's friends coughing but reunited with Bayzog's family.

Brenwar was grumbling at Ben and Ben back at him.

Nath sprang like a cat and dashed down. In seconds, he was down inside the valley. "What is it? What is wrong?"

Ben had one arm and Brenwar had the other of a lone man who stood between them. A hood was crushed in Brenwar's free hand. The man had tattoos on his bald head and face. His teeth were grey and crooked.

"Ah," the acolyte said, licking his teeth, "you must be Nath Dragon. I've a message for you from the great Gorn Grattack himself. These friends are delivered as agreed. But your other friend, Gorlee the Deceiver? Well, if you want him, then you'll have to get him yourself. All by yourself, that is. Heh heh heh!"

Fallen Foes: Faylan and Finlin

CHAPTER 36

"**Y**OU THINK IT'S FUNNY, DO you?" Brenwar leveled the acolyte with a fist to the gut.

Whop!

The man doubled over and fell to his knees.

"What happened, Brenwar?"

"Magic," Bayzog intervened, "a well-crafted illusion. It seems we've been deceived."

Nath looked at Sasha.

She was meek and disheveled, as were her sons. "It's me, Nath," she said, hugging Bayzog. "All me and my sons. Thank you, Nath. You didn't have to do that, but I'm glad you did."

Nath stepped over and stretched his long arms around them both. "So am I."

The happy reunion was short. They all headed up the hillside, back into the barn. Inside, Nath had no doubt he'd done the right thing, giving up Fang as ransom for his friends. But there was another surprise when they returned. Selene was gone.

Brenwar and Pilpin dragged the acolyte into the barn and shackled him up in the moorite chains.

"Hah, I'm honored," the greasy cleric said. "All this trouble over little me. I always knew I was a large threat. Gorn will be pleased."

"Shaddup!" Brenwar said. He started to stuff a handkerchief in the man's mouth.

"Oh, I wouldn't do that. I have something to say. Something you must hear today, before it's too late."

Pilpin shoved the man's head back into the post.
Conk!

"Spit it out, then."

Blinking and rolling his eyes, the cleric finally looked up at Nath. "Your changeling friend will die at the last light. That's not long from now, Nath Dragon. Go soon, and go by yourself. Gorn will free your friend, and then the two of you can be alone."

Nath kneeled down. "Is that all of your message?"

The acolyte's eyes brightened. "It certainly is."

Fuming, Nath flicked the man's chin with his index finger, rocking his head back and knocking him out cold. He rose, headed outside the barn, and spied the Floating City. The setting sun was reflecting off the windows.

Bayzog glided to Nath's side. "It seems your hand is being forced. Doing what he wants you to will be a bad move." Bayzog laid his hand on Nath's shoulder. "You've been patient thus far; don't be hasty now. We'll think of something."

"I've done enough thinking. The time has come to act." Nath surveyed his surroundings. His dearest friends were there. Dozens of dragons huddled nearby, perhaps more inside the hillsides. "Everyone gather."

His friends crowded around him, and many dragons slunk inward.

"I want to thank you all for being here for me. No dragon could ask for a better group of friends, but I have to do what must be done. I have to face our mortal enemy one on one, and I am ready." He glanced down at Brenwar. "Do not interfere." He took Brenwar's hand inside his. "There is no one I'd rather have by my side in this battle, Brenwar, but you know it cannot be."

Brenwar grumbled, but nodded his head.

"I'm going into that city to end this war, but I need you around to finish it in case I can't." He made his way around the circle and hugged each and every one of them. He stopped at Sasha and wiped away the tears that rolled down her cheeks.

She hugged him tight, sobbing and saying, "Don't go. Don't go yet. Gorlee will understand."

Nath shook his head no. "Gorn will just pick off one friend after another. I have to put an end to this madness now." He released her and stepped away. Channeling his power, he made dragon wings sprout from his back. He beat them and lifted off the ground. "Remember, no one does anything until you know Gorlee is safe, or I am gone."

The higher he rose, the smaller his friends became.

Then he heard Ben's strong voice shout into the sky, "Take it to him, Dragon, like I know you can!"

Brenwar watched his flying friend turn into a speck and disappear into the Floating City. His stubby fingers clawed at his beard. "How in Nalzambor does he stand a chance against those odds? There's a thousand jaxite-controlled dragons in there, not to mention Gorn Grattack. Pah!" He punched his fist into his hand. "It's madness."

"I don't know how he beats those odds, but have some faith in him, why don't you?" added Ben. "I believe, and you should believe as well."

"I'd believe better if I could get in there with my war hammer."

The dragons stirred, squawked, and beat their wings.

Sansla Libor took to the sky. The Roamers unsheathed their blades.

"Someone comes," Rerry said, eyeing the crest of the road that led down to the farm. "Look."

Brenwar's eyes went wide, and his fingertips turned numb. A waving dark banner of black and gold appeared on the horizon.

CHAPTER

38

Soaring through the sky, Nath Dragon stretched out his arms. There was nothing more liberating than the sound of the wind rushing by his ears. Heading to his doom or not, the feeling was exhilarating.

His wings beat, slow and powerful. He circled the remains of Quintuklen below. Every tower, every spire was rubble. The walls—which circled the city in a labyrinth—were half torn down. They were of little use against flying dragons.

Men scurried from broken building to broken building. Survivors. Even though Quintuklen was in ruin, most people would not abandon their homes until they died. The sight of the desperate scavengers stirred Nath's heart and angered him. What gave Gorn the right to take homes away from anyone?

He swooped through the air and sped toward the ominous bulk of the Floating City, which hung like a dreadnought in the sky. Nath carefully weighed his thoughts. He could accept Gorlee's sacrifice. After all, he would do the same. He could muster an army of men, dwarves, and dragons and attack the forces of Barnabus like a juggernaut, but how many more would die? Thousands? Tens of thousands? He made his decision.

Better one of me than all of thee.

Bearing down on the city, a lone figure dropped to his side. It was the feline fury.

"Away now," he said in Dragonese, pointing at the cat. "It's my fight alone."

The cat dragon's eyes narrowed as it growled in response and veered away.

Nath watched it go, realizing the fury didn't even have a name.

If I survive this, I'll take care of that. It's something Selene should have done.

Ahead, the dragons stretched their necks from their perches and crowed. The Floating City was still spinning, pulled by the dragons shackled by the neck. Nath clenched his fists. It fired his furnaces within. Smoke rolled from his nose, and his golden eyes smoldered. He cut through the building tops, whizzed over the streets. Dragons hissed and coiled. Armies of the undead gathered in the streets, pressing around the large cathedral-type building he remembered from his visit here.

Nath landed on the stairs.

Armored skeletons and dragons of all sorts crowded near with their eyes glowing. Armor rustled and dragons hissed and slithered.

It rankled Nath, their hatred. Evil. He turned his back on them and placed his hands on the massive doors. His heart thundered inside his chest.

This is it, Dragon. This is it.

A thought lingered in his mind.

Selene. Will she be at Gorn Grattack's side? Was this the plan all along?

Weaponless aside from his dragon claws and magic, he shoved the massive doors open.

Gorn Grattack waited inside. His monstrous voice echoed as he spoke. "Come. Come and die."

Nath stepped within, and the door shut behind him.

Thoom!

Massive cauldrons of fire illuminated the room. Windows stained in dark colors let little sunlight show through. There were cages, empty ones, scattered throughout the room. The smell of death and decay lingered. Fang was nowhere in sight. Neither was Gorlee. Selene, to his relief, was nowhere either.

Nath's scales tingled. Cried out.

Danger!

In front of him once again waited his greatest enemy. Seated on a throne of stone was the foul foe of Nalzambor. Gorn towered ten feet tall. He was covered in brawn and greyish scales. Razor-sharp horns crowned his head, and his eyes had an evil glow.

"Nothing to say, Nath Dragon?"

"Where is my friend Gorlee?"

"Ah, I see," Gorn said, holding his chin. "You still are concerned about these mortals. Tsk. Tsk. Tsk. Such a weakness."

"Where is he?" Nath demanded.

"You do realize it's only a matter of time until all of your *friends* are dead, don't you?" Gorn folded his arms over his chest. "I control most of the dragons in this world. Only a small remnant of free dragons remains. A paltry force stands against me at best. I control the jaxite, and this city is shielded from the attacks of mortals. Why, I even have your precious sword. Once I finish you, I'll melt it down. Then I'll wipe out all of my enemies—the elves, dwarves, and those pesky Roamers—and it will be onward to my Mountain of Doom."

"You might defeat me, but you won't defeat my father. You couldn't the last time."

"Hah! Your father withers while I grow stronger." Gorn clenched his fists and leaned forward. "He fades from this world. He sent you to fight this battle. A battle he knows he cannot win. You cannot win either. You'll never leave here alive. And all of your friends combined cannot save you. You are doomed, Nath Dragon."

"It's you who are doomed."

"Really, how so? I'm in control of everything."

"If that were the case, then I wouldn't be here to fight you now."

"Ah, so you are ready to battle, then? You look ill prepared in your current form." Gorn showed an oversized smile of dragon teeth. "You might want to try bigger, like me." He stood up, and his form increased. From the other side of the room, he sneered down at Nath. "You don't stand a chance."

"Release my friend!"

Gorn reached behind the throne, grabbed something, and brought it forward. It was Fang. "This friend?" Gorn pulled it from the sheath, revealing the bright glow of the blade. The scales on that hand sizzled and smoked. "Isn't that quaint?" he snorted. "It doesn't seem to like me. I can handle that."

Nath's eyes narrowed as he drifted closer.

Gorn studied the blade as he squeezed it with his monster-sized, clawed hand.

Fang's blade hummed and throbbed with light, turning from a bright golden sheen to blue as night before fading to a dark blackish purple. The hilt stopped smoking.

Gorn Grattack laughed. "That was easy." He shrugged. "There is nothing I cannot control in this world. It all lives and dies under my command." He raised the sword high. "I'll make this interesting." He jammed the blade down into the throne. "If you want it, come and take it."

"I didn't come for Fang. I came for Gorlee."

Gorn sighed. "So be it then. Draykis!"

Two winged draykis emerged from the dark beneath the balconies, dragging a figure. The pinkish form of Gorlee sagged between them, head dangling. They dropped him on the floor in front of Gorn and departed.

"Yes, Nath, your friend, the changeling," Gorn said as he started to snicker, "is dead."

Nath's face turned blood red.

"Nooooooooooooooooooooooooo!"

CHAPTER
39

"IT CAN'T BE." BRENWAR SLUNG his war hammer over his back.

"It is," Bayzog said.

The waving black and gold banner showed a hammer and anvil. Another banner appeared, showing a sun shining over a land of blues and old gold. A stout dwarf in plate armor from the neck down carried the black and gold banner of the dwarves. An elven warrior wearing a green tunic over a suit of chain mail carried the other banner. Behind them, twelve dwarves and twelve elves came.

"Haarviik!" Brenwar shouted out.

A dwarf bigger than Brenwar marched forward and clasped his hand. He wore heavy armor, and his lustrous beard was more white than brown.

Haarviik was one of the highest commanders of Morgdon. Higher than Brenwar, even.

"Great to see you, old warrior," Haarviik said. "No other dwarf I'd rather fight beside at the end."

"Are the armies with you?" Brenwar said, peering over Haarviik's shoulder.

"Nay, certainly you would have heard them marching if they were."

"Aye, there's no sound greater than dwarven boots. But your voice will have to do." He slapped Haarviik's shoulder. "So, what can you share with me?"

A tall elf made his way over. His silvery light armor gleamed in the sunlight. His helm of hammered leaves twinkled. He offered his hand to Brenwar, who shook it, then to Bayzog.

"Your arrival is both pleasing and surprising, Laedorn," Bayzog said.

"Greetings," Laedorn said, making a slight bow. "We've marched day and night." His gaze drifted toward the Floating City. "And I believe our timing is just right." His light-green eyes scanned the farm. "Where is Nath Dragon?"

"You just missed him. He's taken to the Floating City. I could not delay him," Bayzog said.

"That is unfortunate," Laedorn said. "But we must not tarry."

"The time to strike is now," Haarviik grumbled. "Now, they won't be looking."

"What are you getting at?" Brenwar said, scowling. "You said you don't have an army. Only two score warriors are with you. Did the elves bring magic ropes and ladders to climb into that spinning city? No disrespect, but I say, 'Hah!'"

"It's ready, isn't it?" Bayzog said to Laedorn.

"What's ready?" Brenwar said.

"The weapon," Haarviik said to Brenwar. He clasped Brenwar's shoulder. "The one we've been working on."

Brenwar's eyes went wide. "I thought you only had two of the three pieces."

"We did, but now we have the third."

"Bayzog, what is your understanding of all this?" Brenwar said.

"I know little more than you, but I know this is a dangerous plan, only to be used as a last resort. I don't think we are there yet. What has changed, Laedorn?"

Laedorn motioned toward the troops. The elves and dwarves marched forward with their packs. Each carried several metal pieces marked with intricate patterns. Quickly, they got to work assembling a contraption that pointed at the Floating City. Busy dwarven hands tightened large bolts with metal wrenches. Heavy hammers pounded pins in. The elves slid small slivers of metal into place.

"What are they building, Bayzog?" Sasha said with fascination.

"They call it the Apparatus of Ruune."

"What does it do?"

"It destroys things."

"What things?"

Sasha, Rerry, Samaz, and Ben came closer.

"Everything."

"You can't use that when Dragon is in there," Ben objected.

"And they won't," Brenwar added.

"Brenwar," Haarviik said, "our counsels have agreed. It's been almost five hundred years since we've agreed on anything. We will carry out this service."

"You must delay!"

"Oh, we must not, Brenwar Bolderguild," Laedorn said. "And know that my affection for your friends is the same as for my own kin. But we must strike before the opportunity is lost. We've lost many lives hiding the Apparatus and getting it here." Laedorn's chin dipped. "Two of my brothers are gone, among a hundred others. It is agreed we must strike, or thousands more will die. We must smite that city from the sky."

Bayzog approached Laedorn, looking him in the eye. "Why such urgency? You don't even know for certain the amount of power that you wield yet. What if it fails?"

"Urgency is the utmost, Bayzog. Surely you know that. Powerful artifacts are at work here, and it's only a matter of time before Gorn Grattack senses that. His forces will be upon us at any moment. That's why we travel small and discreetly. We cannot appear to pose a threat. And now, with Nath Dragon up there, Gorn is distracted. This might be our only chance to take him."

"And risk killing our friends? Nay!" Brenwar said. "Give him more time!"

Laedorn sighed. "We can't put our fate in the hands of the dragons, just as the dragons cannot put their fate in ours. We must act."

Brenwar's eyes slid over to the Floating City. Bright lights flashed. Something was stirring. He shook his head. "Give him more time."

"Once the Apparatus is finished, we will unleash all of its fury."

"You can't let them do this, Brenwar," Ben said. "You can't!"

Brenwar grumbled. The Apparatus of Ruune was almost finished. It was a massive cannon standing eight feet off the ground on a tripod of thick iron legs. The elves and dwarves had put large sections of moorite tubes together, wide enough to fit someone's head inside. It was braced down on the tripod, sitting in a bracket that could swivel left to right and up and down. An oversized spyglass was perched on the top. Two seats were lined up behind it. Below it was an iron stomach, a furnace waiting to be fed. There were gears and handles laid out in an intricate array. An oversized stepladder led up into the seats. The marvelous contraption towered over them all.

"You really think this can knock that city out of the sky?" Brenwar said.

"I don't know," Haarviik said, offering a dwarven grin, "but I can't wait to try."

The Apparatus of Ruune

CHAPTER

40

RED WITH ANGER, NATH ROARED. Hot as fire, he summoned his power and charged. Crossing the span between him and Gorn Grattack, he transformed into a full-size dragon.

Gorn lowered his head and shoulders and grew.

The two behemoth dragons collided with a roof-shaking *boom*!

Nath pinned Gorn to the floor and unloaded a blast of green dragon fire.

Gorn's tail slithered around Nath's neck and jerked him away. With a heave, he sent Nath skipping over the tiles.

"You'll pay!" Nath said in an all-powerful dragon voice. "You'll pay for all this!"

Each almost thirty feet tall, the two titans circled, their heads almost grazing the rafters of the massive cathedral.

Ready to spring, Gorn flashed a wicked smile. "You're a fighter, Nath Dragon, but you lack my killer instincts."

Nath said as he charged, "We'll see about that!"

Gorn's eyes bore into Nath's chest, and a blast of purple fire shot from them.

Nath ducked. Fast was good. Big and fast was not the same. The blast caught him in the shoulder and spun him to the tiled cathedral floor. Nath roared and pushed his dragon body upright.

Gorn rammed him with his horns and drove him into the tiles once more. "You are still a boy!"

Whop! Pow! Smash! Smash! Smash!

Gorn's blows were a furious storm. They smote Nath's face, his jaw, his belly. His dragon claws ripped into Nath's scales. Each blow was lightning. Each impact was power.

Wham! Wham! Pop! Crack!

Nath felt Gorn's clawed hands wrapped around his neck. Claws dug in. He was being choked to death.

No. No. No. Nooooooooo!

With a powerful blast from his eyes, Nath let loose the furnace within.

The white-hot blast snapped back Gorn's head, and Gorn's fingers loosened around Nath's neck.

Nath gathered his legs between them and thrust with all his power into Gorn's belly. The Dragon

Warlord was catapulted through the air, blasting through the roof and onto the streets.

Nath sprang to his feet, gathered his breath, and crashed through the great doors of the cathedral. Gorn lay in the street holding his head. At least a dozen skeleton warriors were crushed beneath him.

He rushed Gorn again.

A sky raider dropped between them. A blast of fire came from its mouth, catching Nath in the chest.

He stormed right through it and locked his arms around the sky raider's neck. "Are you fighting this battle yourself or not, Gorn?"

Gorn staggered up and waved the crowding dragons aside. "It's just me and you!"

Nath popped the sky raider in the jaw and slung it away. "No," he responded. "It's just me!" He pounced on Gorn and started hammering away, one heavy blow after the other.

Pow! Pow! Pow! Pow! Pow!

The two of them slammed through the streets and tore through the city. The buildings shook. Glass shattered. Ancient statues toppled over. The entire city trembled. The pair of titans thrashed back and forth. Nath pressed with punches. Gorn flailed back with his tail. Nath drove Gorn through building after building. He pummeled his enemy down.

Whop!

Gorn's dragon head crashed with Nath's fist and into the street. Nath's chest was heaving.

Gorn started laughing. "Ha ha ha! You tire already, and I haven't even begun fighting."

"Neither have I," Nath gasped.

Whop!

He punched Gorn.

Gorn got bigger.

Pow!

Gorn got bigger.

Wham! Wham! Wham!

Gorn got bigger and bigger and bigger. The monstrous dragon lord shoved Nath aside like a doll and rose to his full height.

Shoulders sagging, Nath looked up and swallowed.

Gorn stood more than fifty feet tall. He was almost twice the size of Nath. Bigger than most buildings. "You are such a fool, Nath Dragon! My power is ten times yours. Now taste what true power is!" He open his mouth, and a blast of dark-purple fire came out.

The scale-blistering heat made Nath let out an awful blood-curdling roar. "Bah-Ha-Rooooooooooooo!" He fell to his hands and knees. He couldn't breathe. Coated in excruciating flames, he was suffocating. The roar of flames was deafening, the unbearable heat terrifying. Stunned, he couldn't think. He couldn't counter.

Hang on, Nath Dragon! A voice inside his head said. *Hang on!*

Who said that? Was it him? Was it his father?

The flames stopped. Smoke rolled off his cooling scales. But the pain was still there. Mind-numbing pain. It was bad, but not as bad as Gorn's laughter.

"How is that for a baptism by fire, Nath Dragon? Torture, isn't it?" Gorn reached down and lifted up Nath's chin. "That is what is in store for the rest of the world, and it seems there is nothing you can do about it. Ha! You are not ready yet. You could have been if you were patient and let your friends die, but you chose their lives for your death. How fitting for a fool."

Gorn released him and let out a triumphant sigh. He slithered his great neck from side to side and bared his razor-sharp claws and teeth. "Now it's time to pluck your beating heart out, one scale at a time." He stepped around Nath and grabbed his tail. "But let's soften you up a bit more first."

Eyes swollen shut, Nath felt himself being dragged through the streets. He heard the dragons taunting him and praising Gorn. All of his strength had evaporated. Where had it gone?

I'm beaten. But I can't be beaten. I can't be!

Gorn slung him like a club into the buildings, one right after the other, and then dragged him back inside what was left of the cathedral.

CHAPTER

41

"IT'S READY," LAEDORN SAID, SLIDING a small pack off his back and setting it on the ground. Haarviik did the same. The packs were made of a pale green elven wool that had a soft glow to it. "Within lie the Thunder Stones. Once we load them in the Apparatus of Ruune, we must unleash their power without delay."

"I thought you said there were three of them," Bayzog said, rubbing his neck. "Who carries the third?"

"I do," said a strong female voice. Selene waded through the elves and dwarves and stood among them. A stone wrapped up in dark crimson cloth filled her hands. "I'd been saving it for other plans, but now it is yours to master."

Bayzog waded in closer as they unwrapped the stones. His skin tingled. His heart flinched. Such power would make him or anybody invincible. He took a deep breath and found Selene staring at him.

The corner of her lip was turned up in a smile. "Tempting, isn't it, Bayzog?"

He wasn't sure what to make of her, or any of them for that matter. This historic alliance was strange indeed. It seemed the elves, led by Laedorn, had chosen to save her with the Ocular of Orray. But had they done it so she could help Nath Dragon, or had they done it because they needed her help with the Thunder Stones? It was an unlikely unification.

"Yes, it is tempting." His neck hairs prickled. His violet eyes narrowed. "Imagine what you could do with the stones under your power. You would be just as powerful as Gorn Grattack himself." He readied the Elderwood Staff in front of him. "Perhaps that was what you were saving your stone for."

"What are you getting at, Bayzog?" said Brenwar, stepping along his side. "Do you smell treachery among us? Do you doubt her scaly hide?"

Laedorn and Haarviik stopped unwrapping the stones and fixed their eyes on Selene.

Her eyes were aglow. The clawed fingers at her sides flexed and stretched out. Eyes fixed on the stones, she swayed forward.

Bayzog and Brenwar's knuckles whitened on their hilts. There was the scrape of weapons sliding from sheaths. The sounds quieted. The sky turned dim.

"What are you thinking, Selene?" Bayzog said.

Her dark eyes blinked. She shook the locks on her head. "I, I'm thinking it's time to take down Gorn Grattack, but not at the cost of Nath Dragon." She took two steps backward from the stones. "But I will not interfere."

The tension eased, but the doubt in Bayzog's mind remained.

"Laedorn, Haarviik, can you wait another hour? That would be enough time for our friend Gorlee to be released and returned. Perhaps he'll bring news that can be useful."

"Such as?" Haarviik said.

"Such as where in the world do you aim that thing?" Brenwar responded. "Pah. This plan is as bad as an ogre's stench."

"Bayzog!" Sasha exclaimed. "It's Samaz. Look!"

Bayzog whipped around and fastened his eyes on his son, who stood alone and away from the crowd. He's eyes shone a solid white, and he stood with his arms wide and on his tiptoes. He spoke quick words in Elven, repeating the same phrase over and over.

"What is he yammering on about?" Brenwar said to Bayzog. "My Elven is horrible."

"He comes," Bayzog said, glancing over toward

Laedorn. "Fire the weapon. He comes. Fire the weapon."

"We can no longer hesitate," Laedorn said. He filled his hands unwrapping his stone. It was pearl in color with ancient gold runes engraved on it. Inside, it beat with mystic life.

Haarviik unwrapped his stone. It was a marble rock with red runes engraved on it. A red glow pulsated inside.

"Take the third," Selene said to Bayzog. "They'll need your wizard's touch for this."

Bayzog hesitated, then ambled over. He picked the stone up off the ground. The power he felt enlightened him from fingertip to toenail. Elation. Exhilaration. Temptation. His violet eyes flashed. A struggle within ensued. The vibrant man inside him collided with his pious elven self. A storm raged.

Laedorn and Haarviik, radiating power, lugged their stones toward the apparatus and fed them into its iron belly. Up the ladder they went, from there to take the bench seat behind the cannon. Haarviik grabbed the handles and turned the many bare gears. The Apparatus of Ruune's barrel shifted over, rose, and aimed at the Floating City. The old dwarf eyed the line of sight and nodded. The elf and dwarf each slipped on a pair of leather goggles.

"It's time, Bayzog," Laedorn said. "Unwrap yours and load it."

Bayzog felt his heart thumping in his ears. Could the weapon destroy everything inside the city? Nath would die, Gorlee would die, and hundreds of dragons who had been turned to the evil side would die. He glanced over at Sasha. Tears stood in her eyes, but her warm, pretty face had no answers. He turned away and removed the cloth from the stone. It was onyx marked with silver runes. He stepped over to the contraption and opened the door to its stomach. Inside, the pair of Thunder Stones throbbed in unison, beckoning for the third. Trembling, Bayzog set it inside the waiting furnace.

The belly glowed with life.

Whuuuuuum!

The ground shook, the trees bent, and Bayzog fell down. A stiff breeze swirled around them all, stirring the hairs on Haarviik and Laedorn's heads. The Apparatus of Ruune hummed a tumultuous tune. A swirl of bright, mystic colors spilled from the barrel.

"Father! Father!" Rerry shouted over the howling winds. He was pointing down the road that led into the valley. "Someone comes!"

The other elves and dwarves pushed Bayzog out of the way. They latched their hands on the apparatus and began chanting.

Whuuuuum!

The sound became louder and louder.

Squinting, Bayzog watched Brenwar and Pilpin rush at the stranger coming up the road. He was waving his hands over his head, staggering as he ran forward. Brenwar and Pilpin cut him off, threw him down, and dragged him forward.

"Who is it?" Bayzog said.

The figure locked eyes with him, blinked, and started to turn. His skin was pinkish. His eyes were wide.

"Gorlee!" Bayzog exclaimed.

Huffing for breath, Gorlee said, "I escaped, but they know you're here and they're coming!" He glanced at the pulsating apparatus. "What is that thing? Where is Nath Dragon?"

"He's in the city!" Bayzog shouted over the wind. "Looking for you!"

"No! No! It's a trap! It's all a big trap! We have to get him out of there!" He tried to pull away, but Brenwar held him fast. "Let go! Let go!"

Bayzog and Brenwar started shouting at Laedorn and Haarviik and waving their arms.

"Stop! Stop!"

Haarviik, beard billowing, shouted, "Cover your ears!" And then with all his dwarven might, he shouted, "Fire!"

Kah—Kah—Kah—Rooooooooooom!

A bright ball of energy blasted out of the barrel and soared through the sky. Bayzog watched in awe. The blue-green torpedo of energy was on a direct path into the very heart of the city. Bayzog sank to his knees. Sasha huddled at his side, watching with dread-filled anticipation. He barely heard the words she said.

"Balzurth be with you, Nath."

CHAPTER
42

A PUMMELING. A BEATDOWN. NATH FELT like a child fighting a man. Gorn was bigger. Gorn was stronger. It took everything Nath had to keep himself together.

He can't be this powerful. He can't be!

Gorn wailed on him. He felt every blow in his bones. He struck back only to be swatted aside and assaulted again.

"I can't kill you this way, but I enjoy delivering the pain!"

Nath, sprawled out on the ground, struggled to rise.

Gorn kicked him in the gut. Blasted him with more fire.

"That's for your father! And after I finish you, I'll finish him!"

Gorn drove his fist into him and kicked him once more.

Listless and wrought with pain, Nath lay on his back in the supine position as Gorn walked away. He'd hardly put up a fight. He was ashamed of it. It angered him. Selene had told him to hold back his powers, and as far as he could tell, he'd exhausted them all. Gorn's powers seemed unlimited. They seemed to be growing. What was feeding the monster that made him so strong? He heard a voice inside his head.

Fear and doubt are our enemies. Evil feeds on them.

Bayzog had said that.

Sometimes you have to set your faults aside and be a hero.

Brenwar had lectured that.

Nothing can stop Nath Dragon.

Nath rose to his feet with a groan and pulled his shoulders back.

"I said that."

"What's this?" Gorn said, stomping over the throne where Fang was embedded. "Still some fight in you, I see. Hah hah hah!" Gorn plucked the tiny sword from the chair. "Let me show you true power, my full power."

Fang sparkled and hissed in his palms and began to enlarge.

Nath's golden eyes widened. "Impossible!"

225

"You think small, Nath Dragon. And with your precious sword, I'm going to sliver off your scales and skewer your heart."

Nath crouched back. He felt more odds stacking against him.

How is he doing this? What can't he do? Think, Nath. Think.

"You'd think you'd have your own sword," Nath said. "Sad thing you have to use mine. It seems you lack many skills my father has."

Gorn sprang across the room and swung Fang at his belly.

Slice!

Nath skipped away.

Guzan! That was close.

Gorn jabbed Fang at him again and again.

Nath twisted, ducked, and dodged. The cathedral was collapsing all around him.

"Stay still, you fool!"

Nath did no such thing. Gorn thrust. He moved. Gorn jabbed. He sidestepped. He narrowed his eyes. *Nothing is faster than Nath Dragon.* His dragon heart surged inside his chest, his confidence renewed. Gorn cut and chopped. He anticipated and moved.

Evil is overconfident.

Brenwar had once said that.

The wicked are powerful but often sluggish.

Bayzog's memory reminded.

Nath felt his senses coming together now.

Wary, Gorn waded through the city. He'd close in on Nath, only to see him slip away time and again.

"I tire of this!" Gorn growled. He looked up into the spires. "Dark dragons, pin him down!"

The dragons spread their wings and dropped from the sky.

Nath acted. He summoned his power and unleashed a cone of icy dragon breath.

Distracted, Gorn slipped on his next step and thudded into the street.

Nath unleashed his full fury, freezing Gorn's legs and covering his chest and arms.

The dragons flew at him and latched onto his arms and legs.

He slung them off and pounced on Gorn Grattack.

Fang was frozen to Gorn's hands.

Nath tried to pry him out.

"Ha!" Gorn said from his frozen cocoon. "You think to fool me, do you? Admirable try, but my grip is solid iron." Flexing his scales, Gorn busted the ice off. He slugged the gaping Nath in the jaw with the hilt of his own sword. "Fool!"

Smaller dragons clawing all over him, Nath crashed to the ground. "No!"

Gorn was on his feet towering over him with Fang resting on his shoulder.

Nath strained against his living coat of dragon armor. They had him pinned. Gorn had him right where he wanted him.

Nath's father's words entered his head.

Evil is deceitful. Don't close your mind for a second.

"Let go of me, brothers and sisters! You don't know what you're doing!"

"Save your breath, Nath. They don't listen to you, they listen to me." Gorn readied Fang over his head. "They listen to me from now on, forever!" He started into his swing.

BOOOOOOOOOM!

The entire Floating City shook. Nath felt it tilt beneath him. Above, some sort of meteor skipped off a mystic shield he hadn't noticed before. Gorn stumbled backward, and a sneer formed on his lips. He opened his mouth to speak again.

BOOOOOOOOOM!

The Floating City trembled again.

"Dragons!" he roared. "Find that weapon and destroy it!"

Dragons by the hundreds took to the sky, darting through the shield and away.

Gorn leered down at Nath. "I suspected such a thing, but I control the jaxite's power. Nothing but dragons can get in or out of this city." He waggled Fang in the air. "The more dragons come, the more I control. And in moments, those distant heroes, no matter their force, will be torn into pieces." He readied the sword for the final blow once more. "Don't worry, Nath Dragon. You'll never get to see it."

CHAPTER

43

A S HE WATCHED THE MAGIC torpedo fly, Brenwar's chest tightened. Thoughts of not seeing Nath again raced through his mind. As the great missile sailed up, he ground his teeth and braced his mind for impact.

Behind him, everyone watched with rapt fascination.

Brenwar's keen eye caught a quavering bubble that he hadn't noticed before. It surrounded the city.

"Great Guzan! What is that? A shield? Bayzog, do you see that?"

The mage squinted.

Careening through the sky, the bright blast sailed toward the city, barreling down on the mass of buildings. There was a bright flash followed by a thunderous boom. An invisible dome appeared, saving the city. The ball of power skipped off the greenish dome and skittered into the sky before fading.

"Buckle my boot! It ricocheted!" Brenwar yelled. He felt relief. He turned back toward Haarviik. "*Now* what are you going to do?"

Haarviik stood up in his seat and pulled up his leather goggles. His weathered face was painted with fury. "It cannot be!"

Suddenly, coming out of the Floating City, dragons by the hundreds filled the sky. Black tailed and winged with glowing eyes, they soared straight for the Apparatus of Ruune.

"Fire again!" Haarviik bellowed, plopping down in his seat. "Fire!"

Laedorn and Haarviik pulled back on their triggers and let chaos fly.

Kah—Kah—Kah—Rooooooooooom!

Kah—Kah—Kah—Rooooooooooom!

Kah—Kah—Kah—Rooooooooooom!

Torpedoes ripped through the dark dragons, incinerating them before blasting into the dome protecting the city. But the blast only took a few of the hundreds that remained. The dragons swarmed toward them, roaring in fury.

"Pilpin, fetch the chest!" Brenwar yelled.

"Aye!" Pilpin said, scurrying into the barn.

The Apparatus of Ruune continued to rock, blast after blast after blast.

Kah—Kah—Kah—Rooooooooooom!
Kah—Kah—Kah—Rooooooooooom!
Kah—Kah—Kah—Rooooooooooom!

The torpedoes destroyed dragons in their path but continued to ricochet off the dome.

Bayzog appeared at his side. "They'll be on us at any moment. What do you plan to do?"

Brenwar cocked his eyebrow. "Fight! One last glorious fight!"

A series of roars erupted behind them. The good dragons who had been huddled in the hills took to the sky and surged toward the oncoming enemy. Brenwar could see that the good dragons were outnumbered at least four to one.

"When they get here, they'll rip that apparatus apart," Bayzog said, "and then it will be over. We have to protect it!"

"I thought you didn't like it?" Brenwar said.

"Quite the contrary. It's fascinating. I just don't like Nath being on the other end of it."

Pilpin scurried back with the dwarven chest in his arms. He set it down and peeled the ancient lid open. Bayzog kneeled down and started plucking out vial after vial. He tossed them to his family, the Roamers, Ben, and Pilpin.

"Just drink," Brenwar said, pulling the cork off one and draining it down. "No time for questions." He thumped his chest and burped. Eyeing a hesitant Pilpin, he said, "If I can drink, you can drink."

Pilpin gave a quick bearded nod and swallowed the greenish potion down.

"Everyone, form a circle around the apparatus and stay close," Bayzog said. He stepped underneath the weapon's muzzle and readied the Elderwood Staff. "Have faith this isn't the end."

Kah—Kah—Kah—Rooooooooom!

Kah—Kah—Kah—Rooooooooom!

Dragons tore at one another. The sky was filled with firework-like destruction: lightning, fire, black acid, streams of lava, smoky eruptions. Dragons big and small battled for it all. Wings were torn and shredded. Dragons fell like great scaled birds from the air. Once so beautiful and majestic, now they were razor-clawed, fire-breathing terrors. The roars of battle were angry, painful, deafening. It was mayhem. Carnage.

"Stay close to me," Bayzog said to his wife Sasha, "no matter what."

"I will." Rising up on her tiptoes, she kissed his cheek. "But I have to admit, I feel great. What potion did you give me?"

He looked into her eyes. They were aglow with radiant fire. Her hands tingled with mystic life in his. "One that will increase your powers."

"How much?"

"Did you drink the entire thing?"

"Yes."

He showed a little smile. "Five-fold at least. But remember, its effects are only temporary. "

Sasha faced the oncoming wave of dragons in the sky and clenched her charged-up fist. "Then temporary will just have to do. It's time to let those rotten lizards have it!"

Bayzog summoned the power of the Elderwood Staff. The gemstone carved into the ancient wood flared with brilliant tangerine light. It fed him. Empowered him. His eyes smoldered with mystic light.

"Everyone!" Bayzog yelled. "Don't strike until you see the green of their eyes!"

The clamor of battle in the sky subsided. The swarm of steel-hard, dark-scaled beasts would be on them at any moment. Bayzog heard Brenwar cry out.

"What are you waiting for, Haarviik? Get to firing that thing!"

Bayzog turned and looked. Something was wrong. Laedorn and Haarviik were frozen.

Selene! he thought. *Where is Selene?*

CHAPTER
44

NATH'S MIND WAS A RACE of thoughts. Gorn
loomed over him with his beloved sword
Fang, whose keen blade reflected dark powers.
All over Nath, dragons pinned him down. They'd
latched onto his legs, his arms. Tails encircled his
neck, ankles, and wrists. Other dragons, strange
ones of a dark-green hue, bit into his body with a
leech-like quality. They drained his power.

He groaned. He strained.

For decades he'd fought to save them, only to
see them destroying him. His friends would die
as well. Gorn was right. He didn't want to see it.
So many things he considered that he didn't even
notice the blade descending.

Booooooooooooooom!

Booooooooooooooom!

More blasts shook the city. Gorn lost his

balance. The sword missed its mark, cleaving into a copper dragon, who exploded.

Nath swallowed the lump in his throat.

That was close!

Gorn held his free clawed hand up in the air and said with venom, "Perhaps I should rip your heart out of your chest myself!"

Nath started to reply, but, choking, he couldn't speak. But another voice did.

"I wouldn't do that."

Gorn's head twisted to the side. A dragon, lavender and white scaled, stood nearby. It was Selene.

"You!" Gorn said. "Impossible!"

"Oh, Gorn, you should know better than that. After all, you came back from the brink of death. Why can't I?"

He huffed a blast of fire at her feet, but she remained still. "What game are you playing, Selene?"

Her magnificent lavender wings spread out and fluttered, then folded behind her back. She was as captivating as a dragon as she ever had been as a woman. Her eyes were dark-purple gems, pretty. She batted her lashes.

"I've brought you a gift," she said.

"A gift," Gorn growled. "What sort of gift?"

Nath couldn't believe his eyes. His ears. Selene had betrayed him ... again!

She opened up her dragon hands, and bright brilliant light spilled out.

Gorn's eyes widened like moons. "You have the Ocular!" he said, excited.

"It was worth dying for, my lord. And it's all yours."

"You have exceeded my grandest expectations, Selene. My most diabolical plan has come to fruition. You fooled the elves, the dwarves, and Nath Dragon most of all." He belted out a monstrous laugh. "Ha ha ha! You have restored your lost honor."

Her eyes slid over to Nath's before she said, "Sometimes, you just have to have a little faith."

Gorn stretched his fingers out and started to wrap them around the Ocular of Orray. He paused and withdrew.

"A moment, Selene." He turned his attention to Nath. "I have some business to finish first. I'll deal with the Ocular and its uncanny powers next." Once more he towered over Nath. "Do you have anything you would like to say before you perish, Nath Dragon?"

Nath fastened his eyes on Selene. "I have nothing to say. Just kill me."

CHAPTER

45

DRAGON FIRE RAINED DOWN TOWARD the apparatus.

Bayzog unleashed the power of the Elderwood Staff. A powerful arc of energy scattered the ranks of dragons. Beside him, Sasha deflected fire and lightning with shield after shield.

"There's too many!" she yelled.

Dragons landed and rushed.

Two towering figures, more than twenty feet tall, stepped into their path. It was Shum and Hoven. Their Dragon Needles had become gigantic lances. They skewered one dragon after the other. There was smoke and fire, and the dust of battle began to roll. Bayzog heard Brenwar shouting out in the clamor.

"Take that!"

Wham!

"And that!"

Crack!

"And that, you foul lizards!"

Crunch!

"War hammer! War hammer! Hooooooooo!"

A grey scaler, little bigger than him, slid between Shum and Hoven's ranks and charged at Sasha's blind side. Bayzog swung his staff around and connected with its head.

Ka-Koom!

The dragon sagged into the ground, dead, leaving Sasha gasping.

"Are you all right?" he said.

Sasha nodded. "Yes, now keep fighting!"

Wupash!

A dragon tail licked out of the smoke and swept Bayzog from his feet. His head hit hard on the ground.

"Oof!"

A dragon pounced on him, copper scaled and copper eyed. It pinned Bayzog under his staff and snapped at him with its jaws. Its breath was as foul as the acid that dripped from its mouth onto Bayzog's chest.

He moaned. He heard Sasha scream for help. His power ignited. The Elderwood Staff flared, and the copper dragon exploded into ashes.

Chest burning, Bayzog scrambled to his feet. Sasha strained to fend off two grey scalers with her mystic shield. Superior in size and power, the dragons pressed in for a lethal attack. One of the dragons' long tails coiled back to strike. Bayzog wouldn't make it in time.

"Sasha! Watch out!"

A blur whizzed by Bayzog and sliced into the nearest dragon. It was Rerry. His body and blades moved at impossible speeds. He was a whirling dervish of flashing steel. The grey scaler growled and hissed as Rerry ripped through his scales.

Slice! Slice! Slice! Slice! Slice!

"Get away from my mother, dragon!" Rerry cried out.

On the other side, a bulk fell out of the sky, landed on the other dragon's neck, and wrestled it to the ground. It was Samaz. He punched at the dragon with fists made of iron. With tremendous punches, he pummeled the beast into submission.

Whop! Whop! Whop!

Bayzog caught Sasha up in his arms. Her forehead was beaded in sweat. All around them was the clamorous chaos of battle.

"Can you still fight?" he said to her.

"I still have plenty left in me, I've just never fought two dragons before." She squinted. "And these dragons better not hurt my boys." Her hands charged up with blue light. She summoned a fireball and hurled it at a dragon engaged with Rerry. The blast knocked off its scales.

"Mother!" Rerry said. "I'm a big elf! I can take care of myself!" In a flash of speed, he assaulted another.

Whump!

A sky raider landed on top of the barn, crushing it to splinters. Another one landed behind it, followed by another. There was enough fire in them to lay waste to the farm in one breath.

"Everyone to me!" Bayzog yelled. "Everyone now!"

The giants Shum and Hoven kept fighting the dragons that hung all over them. They both bled from at least a dozen wounds. Valiant. Unfailing.

Bayzog heard the first sky raider taking in a breath. Any second, it would wipe them out. Then, out of the sky, a blur of fur and muscle appeared.

Sansla Libor, fists ready, flew into the dragon and smote him in the face with ram-like force.

Another figure ran through the streets toward the sky raiders, getting bigger with every stride. It was Gorlee, transforming into a giant made of stone. He tackled the sky raider and drove it to the ground. The other sky raiders pounced Gorlee the Stone Giant. They attacked with fire and claws.

"No!" Bayzog yelled. "Come back! Come back to me!"

Shum, Hoven, Sansla, and Gorlee kept fighting. So did Samaz and Rerry, close by.

"Samaz! Rerry! To me!"

The sons broke off their attack and hurried back to their parents. Bayzog jammed the butt of his staff to the ground.

Wuh-Wuuuuuuuuuum!

A mystic yellow dome formed around them and the apparatus, protecting them, with a few dragons inside.

Sasha unleashed her power on the dragons.

Sssraz! Ssssraz! Sssraz!

Rerry and Samaz cut and pounded down the others.

Slice! Whop! Slice! Whop! Slice!

Rerry stuck his tongue out at Samaz. "I whipped many more than you."

"Wizard!" Brenwar said, emerging from behind the apparatus with Pilpin. The pair were bloody and battered. "What do we do?"

Dragons, eyes glowing green, pressed the mystic dome from all over. Bayzog could feel their full weight on him. Sweat dripped down his face.

"I don't know," he said. "I don't know."

His violet eyes darted around their surroundings. The Apparatus of Ruune sat quiet. Laedorn and Haarviik's bodies sat behind it frozen stiff. How could a weapon so powerful fail?

The protective dome began to crack. The dragons were too many. He could only hold them off for seconds longer.

241

Sasha wrapped her arms around his waist and lent him all the strength she had left.

"You did your best, husband. You did your best. Being your wife has been an honor."

Shards of magic cracked away from the shield. His sons joined in the hug as well.

"Keep fighting, Father!" Rerry yelled. "Keep fighting!"

Bayzog found new strength, and a desperate thought emerged.

"Brenwar!"

"What!"

"Aim the Apparatus of Ruune at the jaxite!"

"Then what?"

"Fire it!"

Pilpin scrambled up the ladder and shoved Laedorn and Haarviik out of their seats.

"Sorry, Commanders."

Brenwar huffed up behind him.

More shards of energy fell. Dragon horns pounded through the mystic dome. Dragons squirmed through.

"Hurry, Brenwar! Hurry!"

Pilpin and Brenwar worked the gears with the handles, and Brenwar yelled, "I can't even see what I'm aiming at!"

"Just do your best for the love of Morgdon and fire!"

Assault on the Floating City

CHAPTER

46

"I T'S OVER," GORN SAID. "NALZAMBOR will be mine forever!"

Nath, straining with all his might, gave one final heave against the dragons. The effort was futile. He glared at Selene. "You picked the wrong side."

"Oh, did I?" she replied with a smirk on her face.

Fang flashed in the sun.

Selene spoke a word of power, and the Ocular of Orray burst with brilliant blinding light.

"Argh!" Gorn said, staggering back and covering his eyes in his elbow. "What are you doing, Selene?"

Tendrils of energy stretched out from the Ocular and ripped into the dragons that held Nath down. The dark dragons screamed and scurried. Others darted into the sky, and several suddenly died.

"Ultimate betrayer!" Gorn bellowed. "You shall pay for this!" Gorn blasted Selene with the fire of ten thousand furnaces. It buried her in the buildings, leaving her out of sight beneath a smoking pile of rubble. "Fool!"

Nath sprang to his feet and charged.

Gorn turned on him and swung. The blade sheared through Nath's wing and into his side.

Nath screamed. "Argh!" He blocked out the pain. He kept fighting. He grabbed Gorn's wrists and blasted him in the chest with his own dragon fire. He and Gorn butted horned heads.

Klock! Klock! Klock!

"You are no match for me!" Bigger and stronger, Gorn scooped the exhausted Nath up in one arm and slammed him down hard.

Fang's blade flashed in the sun and came down.

Nath rolled to the side, avoiding a fatal blow that still sank into the meat of him. "Ugh!" He twisted his body around and swept Gorn from his feet with his tail and sprang up, clutching the side of his dragon body. It was bleeding. Bleeding badly. It burned, too. Nothing felt worse than being wounded by a friend. It angered him.

Gorn made his way back to his feet with ease and laughed. "Ha ha ha! Give up, Nath Dragon. I've too much power. I have your sword. The jaxite. Thousands of dragons under my command." He lifted his chin and snorted smoke. "I have more than your father ever had. I am disappointed. It seems you are less of a fighter than he."

"Maybe so," Nath said, "but I'll fight you to the end. This fight isn't over yet." He summoned all of his courage and all of his strength and charged. "Dragon! Dragon!"

Fang licked out faster than a snake's tongue.

Nath stopped short of its tip, spun to one side, and countered with a punch to Gorn's chin.

The Dragon Warlord staggered back and howled.

Nath unleashed radiant beams of fire from his eyes, striking Gorn in the throat.

Again the dragon lord fell back. "I see you learned one of my tricks," Gorn said, "but it will take more than that to save you."

Nath pressed his attack. He brought fire. Rays. Punches. Claws. He gasped in pain with every offensive blow but kept on swinging. He used his speed. All of his energy. He was a hornet stinging a larger enemy.

Gorn chopped one heavy swing after the other. He missed time after time. "Stand still!" Gorn roared. "You annoying fly!"

Nath filled Gorn's face with his dragon fire, but then his inner fires went dim.

Guzan!

He'd used all of his breath up. His body became weak and wobbly.

"Tired," Gorn said, leering down at him, "little dragon?"

Nath punched Gorn in the face with arms that felt like lead.

Gorn unleashed a final blast from his eyes.

Ssssraaaaat!

Nath's body skidded down the street, stopping when he crashed into an ancient fountain. Everything hurt. Everything felt broken. He forced open his swollen eyes. Fifty feet of Gorn towered over him.

What happened?

He'd exhausted his powers and shrunk back down to the size of a man.

"I should squash you like a bug," Gorn said. "But that won't do."

Gasping for his breath, Nath watched Gorn and Fang shrink in size, but he still stood a full ten feet in height.

Gorn reached down, grabbed Nath by the neck, and hoisted him up high. He squeezed Nath's neck in his grip.

Nath kicked his feet, and his face turned beet red, almost purple.

"Oddly silent now isn't it?" Gorn said with a hiss. "The lonely sound of death. Ah, but is that the distant screaming of your friends that I hear? I believe it is. They are dying. But don't fret, Nath Dragon, I'll give all of you a fiery funeral." He rested Fang's tip against Nath's chest. "How nice. I can even feel the last beats of your heart in your chest."

Nath tried to speak, but all he could do was squirm and think about his friends.

Keep fighting until the end.

He felt Fang's tip begin to sink into his scales, but in the distance he heard something else.

Kah—Kah—Kah—Roooooooooom!

"Ah, it seems your friends got off one final shot before they died," Gorn mocked. "A pity it will do neither them nor you any good." He glanced up at the protective dome. "Let's watch the final ricochet together, shall we?"

Nath's golden eyes made their final glance. The magic torpedo soared overhead and kept on going, a shooting star in the night. His heart sank. They'd missed.

Kah—Kah—Kah—Roooooooooom!

A second torpedo skipped off the shield, making a blast of fiery sparks.

He heard another shot and closed his eyes.

"Oh well," Gorn said, "at least they still fight. That's more than I can say for you."

BOOOOOOOOOOOOOM!

The entire Floating City shook so hard that it half tilted over.

"What?" Gorn cried out.

BOOOOOOOOOOOM!

The city shook again, and he dropped Nath on the ground. Out of control, the city started rocking back and forth and spinning in an wobbling fashion.

"Impossible!" Gorn said, shaking his head. "No matter! The end of you is the end of this world."

"You know what your problem is, Gorn?" Nath said, rubbing his neck.

"What might that be, foolish little dragon?"

"You talk too much!" Nath lunged for Fang and jerked Dragon Claw from the hilt. In a flash, he buried the blade in Gorn's chest to the hilt. "And you're too darn slow!"

"No!" Gorn cried out with widening eyes. "Impossible! Nooooooooooo!"

Gorn's body crackled and fizzled, illuminated with light. An eerier cry went out.

Kah-Pooooooooof!

Nath stared down at Gorn's corpse, now turned to bone and ashes that the wind quickly took away. He took Fang from Gorn's disintegrating grip. "I don't ever want to do that again."

Booooooooooooooom!
Booooooooooooooom!
Booooooooooooooom!

Everything was collapsing all around him.

"Selene!"

He rushed over to the pyre where she had last been and dug his claws into the dirt. He found her out cold in the smoking rubble. He took her up in is arms, spread his wings, and took to the sky. His battered wings kept on pumping, barely keeping him aloft. He heard Selene gasp and cough. "Hang in there," he said.

Teetering out of control, the Floating City careened toward the ground. An earth-shaking, horrendous crash smote the mountain tops. The city was destroyed, leaving only giant plumes of smoke and rubble.

Nath said to Selene, "Looks like we did it. We're going to make it."

Her eyes found his. "Of course we are. I had faith, did you?"

CHAPTER
47

THE APPARATUS OF RUNE STOPPED firing. Bayzog's shield collapsed. Dark dragons climbed all over them, the Apparatus, everything. Brenwar swung his hammer into a copper dragon's nose.

Krang!

"Get off me, lizards!"

There was a blinding flash! A thousand bolts of lightning in one.

Boooooooooooooom!

Boooooooooooooom!

Boooooooooooooom!

The dragon surge ended. The dark lizards shook their necks and flapped their wings. The glowing green lights in their eyes went dim.

"Direct hits! Directs hits!" Pilpin said, sliding down the ladder to the smoking barrel of the apparatus. "Look!" he said, waving his arms. "Look!"

The Floating City split into two massive hunks. It teetered and warbled in the sky, sputtering and smoking. Slowly, it drifted toward the earth, dragging the chained dragons down with it.

BAMmmmmm!

It crashed into the mountains with thunderous impact. Smoke billowed up in huge plumes of dust and rubble.

"I'll be," Brenwar exclaimed, mopping the sweat from his brow. "You were right, wizard!" He scanned the area around the apparatus. There were dragons everywhere, some dead, others alive. "Where are you, wizard?"

"Perhaps I can help," Shum said. The giant-sized Roamer elf began picking dragons up from the pile and tossing them aside. Bayzog and his family lay underneath the pile, unmoving.

"Bayzog!" Brenwar jumped off the apparatus and rushed to his friend's side. He scooped him up in his arms. "Wake up, elf! Wake up!"

Bayzog's violet eyes fluttered open. "I was right, wasn't I?"

"About what?"

"Shooting the jaxite."

"It was my shot that did it, elf. Not your advice. Your words had little effect."

Grimacing, Bayzog eyed him, starting to rise. "If you say so, dwarf. Ouch.

"Are you all right?"

"Just a few broken ribs, and possibly my leg. Hardly a wound of note."

"Hah!" Brenwar said, slapping him on the back. "Glad to see I'm finally rubbing off on you. A wizard turned soldier! Too bad the war might be over." He helped Bayzog to his feet, and together they gazed into the sky, where all the bright colors of the rainbow lingered.

Everyone seemed to be all right, especially Rerry.

"What kind of potion did you give me, Father?" Rerry said. "I was so fast!" He jabbed his sword. "Quick!" *Swish!* "My strikes were lightning-filled power! I want to drink that again. Please, please, tell me what it's called."

"In Elven," Bayzog said, "It's called *Cafleiyn*. And no, you can't have any more."

"Aw!"

Gazing toward the distant mountains, Brenwar frowned.

"Do you think he made it?" Bayzog said.

Kabooooom!

Kabooooom!

The Floating City exploded, shaking the ground beneath them.

"What in Nalzambor is that?" Brenwar said.

"The jaxite. Its energy is activated. The Apparatus of Ruune made it unstable."

"We need to get Nath out of there," Brenwar said.

"We need to get us out of here!"

BOOOOOOOOOOOOOOOOOOOOOOOOOOM!

A dome of fiery light covered the mountains. Everyone standing fell from their feet. Dust and debris rained down on them, coating everything.

Coughing, Brenwar stood up and wiped the grit from his eyes, gaping. The mountains were gone. He swallowed hard, and through a cracked voice he said, "I guess that's it then."

Everyone stood in silence.

Tears streamed down Sasha's cheeks.

Pilpin sniffled.

The dragons, of all sorts and colors, made sad honks and drifted away until all of them were gone. Almost an hour passed before Brenwar said, "I suppose we need to go and look for him. Come on, Pilpin."

"Look for who?" someone said.

"Nath," Brenwar grumbled. "Who said that?"

"I did," a voice from above responded.

Every chin tilted upward. Nath hovered in the sky with Selene in his arms.

"You get down here, you ... dragon!"

WEEKS LATER, NATH STOOD INSIDE the throne room at Dragon Home. The piles of gold and treasure were as high as ever. Gemstones twinkled and winked in the grand torchlight. Balzurth sat on the throne, resting his great jaw on his clawed fist.

"Why, you're not even 250 years old," his father said. "You don't really think your days of adventure are over yet, do you?"

"Well, we defeated Gorn Grattack. Stopped the war. What else is there?"

"You don't really think men, elves, orcs, and dwarves are going to start getting along, do you?"

"Well," Nath said, scratching his mane, "I don't suppose, but..." He glanced at Selene.

"Son," Balzurth said, reaching his great clawed hand down and patting him on the head. "You've done so well. But evil never rests. Not only must you be vigilant for all, but also yourself. Don't think for one moment that all the dragons are going to behave."

"I'll keep them in line."

"Ha!" Balzurth's short laugh shook the throne room, loosening the piles of gold like shale. "Just like I kept you in line, eh, Son?" He turned his great frame and head toward the enormous mural in the rear of the throne room. "Every living thing has a mind of its own. Remember that. It's their choice to do right or wrong. Same as it was yours. Same as it will be with your children."

"Children?" Nath said, jaw dropping.

Selene locked her fingers with his.

"You will have children," Balzurth said. "Nothing prepares you for that. They are full of so many wonderful surprises. They can be trouble as well, just as you were to me, I was to my father, and my father to my grandfather. Be firm, just. But always love them, no matter what. "

Balzurth turned his great scaly neck back toward him. His golden eyes were watery. "It's brought me nothing but joy, watching you grow up and become fully dragon, Nath. It aches my heart to have to go, but my time on this world is at its end. I'll see you soon. Never forget how much I love you, Son."

Nath's heart burst in his chest. Tears streamed down his cheeks. He didn't want his father to go.

So much time had been missed, wasted. Now he was going, just like that.

"Don't go, Father! Not yet!"

"Oh," Balzurth said, his eyes brightened.

"Stay for a little longer at least?"

"I wish I could, Nath, but there is an appointed time for all, including me."

Nath fell to his knees and laid his hands on his father's tail. A flood of emotion overcame him. He trembled.

"Son, have no regrets. It's quite natural for the child to leave his parents and live life on his own. We'll be together soon enough on the other side of the mural. Have faith, Son."

Nath sniffed. Even with all the power he'd mastered, he felt like a child once again.

"Father, can you tell me something?" He looked up in Balzurth's eyes. "Was I really hatched from an egg?"

A smile cracked on Balzurth's face. "You need to ask your mother that."

"My mother?" Nath stood. "I really have a mother?"

"Yes, and when I leave, you'll have the power to find her." Balzurth headed closer to the mural.

Nath watched in silence. Stunned, his tongue clove to the roof of his mouth.

With one last wave goodbye, Balzurth slipped into the mural.

"I love you, Father!" Nath blurted out, but Balzurth was already gone.

Nath's chin dipped down to his chest.

Selene rubbed his shoulder.

He patted her hand. "Well," his said, lifting his chin and tossing back his mane. "I guess we should search out my mother."

Selene hugged him and spoke in his ear. "I'll see you later, Dragon King." She kissed his cheek, turned, and headed out of the throne room. The great doors sealed shut behind her.

Nath stood gaping for a while before he climbed up on the throne. There he sat, a dragon-scaled man, fist under his chin on a seat meant for someone ten times bigger than him. He contemplated all he had done. All that had happened. He snapped his fingers, and a ball of flame appeared. With a huff, he blew it out. "I'm bored."

Bong! Bong! Bong!

The pounding on the great doors stirred the piles of coins in the room.

Nath sat up and said, "Open."

The great doors swung inward. The stout, black-bearded figure standing in the threshold seemed so tiny in comparison.

A broad smile formed on Nath's lips. "Brenwar! What are you doing back here?"

In a new set of black plate armor, Brenwar marched into the room and took a knee.

"Rise," Nath said, "and don't ever do that again." He hadn't gotten used to the formalities of being king yet. "Unless you have to. So, what brings you back to visit?"

Brenwar rose to his feet and gazed up at Nath sitting on the throne. "If you get off your hind end and come down here, I'll tell you."

"Oh," Nath said, hopping down out of the massive chair. "Better?"

Brenwar nodded and grumbled, "A little bird called me out. It says to me, 'We need to find Nath the Dragon King's mother.' Unless you'd rather sit on that throne up there."

"You know where she is?"

"I know enough. Are you coming or not, your majesty?"

"Will it be dangerous?"

"Of course."

"Then what are we waiting for?"

AUTHOR NOTES

I just wanted to take a moment to say thanks. Thanks for reading. Thanks for reviewing. Thanks for contacting me and telling me that you liked these stories. It all means so much, and it motivates me.

As for ending a series, well, I hate it. Endings are really, really tough, and I know readers who like the characters will miss reading about them. I'll miss writing them, but remember it's fantasy, so it never really ends. That's why I left some options open at the end. I'd think it's safe to assume at some point, Nath Dragon will return in another series of adventures.

I hope this last book met your expectations. My goal, as always, is to entertain and provide an escape for the reader the best that I can. I want you to have fun but not relax, so you keep turning the pages. As the story was originally designed for younger readers (even though most readers that contact me are much older than I anticipated, which is great), I wanted to adhere the best I could to having a positive message, to stress the importance of trust, friendship, faith, courage, redemption, wisdom, loyalty, and family. I wanted the characters to grow, fight, and overcome the forces of evil. I hope I showed that through the actions of my characters.

Feel free to drop me a line any time, leave a review, and tell me what you think. I always love to hear from you. Your comments are always welcome.

Do good always,

Craig Halloran

Nath meets Sansla Libor (Humor)

ABOUT THE AUTHOR

Craig Halloran resides with his family outside of his hometown of Charleston, West Virginia. When he isn't entertaining mankind, he is seeking adventure, working out, or watching sports. To learn more about him, go to: www.thedarkslayer. com

WORKS BY THE AUTHOR

THE DARKSLAYER: SERIES 1
Wrath of the Royals (Book 1)
Blades in the Night (Book 2)
Underling Revenge (Book 3)
Danger and the Druid (Book 4)
Outrage in the Outlands (Book 5)
Chaos at the Castle (Book 6)

THE DARKSLAYER: SERIES 2
Bish and Bone
Black Blood
Red Death

THE CHRONICLES OF DRAGON
The Hero, The Sword and The dragons (Book 1)
Dragon Bones and Tombstones (Book 2)
Terror at the Temple (Book 3)
Clutch of the Cleric (Book 4)
Hunt for the Hero (Book 5)
Settlements under Siege (Book 6)
Strife in the Sky (Book 7)
Fight and the Fury (Book 8)
War in the Winds (Book 9)
Finale (Book 10)

ZOMBIE IMPACT: SERIES 1
Zombie Day Care: Book 1
Zombie Rehab: Book 2
Zombie Warfare: Book 3

THE SUPERNATURAL BOUNTY HUNTER FILES
Smoke Rising (2015)
I Smell Smoke (2015)
Where There's Smoke (2015)
Smoke on the Water (2015)
Smoke and Mirrors (2015)

Connect with him at:
Facebook – The Darkslayer Report by Craig
Twitter – Craig Halloran

Made in the USA
Lexington, KY
15 February 2015